Frank Richard Stockton

The Associate Hermits

Frank Richard Stockton

The Associate Hermits

ISBN/EAN: 9783337097059

Printed in Europe, USA, Canada, Australia, Japan

Cover: Foto ©Andreas Hilbeck / pixelio.de

More available books at **www.hansebooks.com**

The
Associate Hermits

By

Frank R. Stockton

Author of
"The Great Stone of Sardis"

With Illustrations by

A. B. Frost

NEW YORK AND LONDON
HARPER & BROTHERS PUBLISHERS
1899

BY THE SAME AUTHOR.

THE GREAT STONE OF SARDIS. A Novel. Illustrated by PETER NEWELL. Post 8vo, Cloth, Ornamental, $1 50.

"The Great Stone of Sardis" is as queer and preposterous as can be imagined, yet as plausible and real-seeming as a legal document. . . . There is a treat in the book.—*Independent*, N. Y.

A new and worthy example of Stockton's kindly, wholesome, original, and inexhaustible humor. —*Syracuse Post*.

Narrated with a seriousness that gives the adventures a semblance of matters of fact. Through the narrative runs a love interest which Mr. Stockton manages with great skill.—*Washington Post*.

NEW YORK AND LONDON :
HARPER & BROTHERS, PUBLISHERS.

CONTENTS

CHAPTER   PAGE

    I. The Dawn of a Wedding-Journey   1

   II. Enter Margery   7

  III. Sadler's 15

  IV. A Cataract of Information 23

   V. Camp Rob 35

  VI. Camp Roy 42

 VII. A Stranger 52

VIII. The Bishop's Tale 63

  IX. Matlack's Three Troubles 74

   X. A Ladies' Day in Camp 82

  XI. Margery Takes the Oars 90

 XII. The Bishop Engages the Attention of the

     Guides 100

XIII. The World Goes Wrong with Mr. Raybold 105

 XIV. The Assertion of Individuality 113

  XV. A Net of Cobwebs to Cage a Lion . . . 123

 XVI. A Man who Feels Himself a Man 135

XVII. Mrs. Perkenpine Asserts Her Individuality 143

XVIII. The Hermits Associate 153

 XIX. Margery's Breakfast 161

  XX. Martin Asserts His Individuality 173

CONTENTS

CHAPTER   PAGE

XXI. THE INDIVIDUALITY OF PETER SADLER . . 185

XXII. A TRANQUILLIZING BREEZE AND A HOT WIND 194

XXIII. MRS. PERKENPINE FINDS OUT THINGS ABOUT
HERSELF 205

XXIV. A DISSOLVING AUDIENCE 212

XXV. A MOONLIGHT INTERVIEW 220

XXVI. AN ELOPEMENT 229

XXVII. MRS. PERKENPINE DELIGHTS THE BISHOP . . 239

XXVIII. THE HERMITS CONTINUE TO FAVOR ASSOCIA-
TION 248

ILLUSTRATIONS

THE SUPPER . . . . *Frontispiece*

" ' CAN THIS BE SADLER'S ? ' " . . . . *Facing p* 16

" ' THEY THROW THE OTHER THINGS BACK ' "   "   54

" A LESSON IN FLY-FISHING " . . . . "   80

" BUT THE BISHOP KNEW BETTER " . . . . "   98

" WITH A GREAT HEAVE SENT HIM OUT INTO

     THE WATER " . . . . "   102

" ' WHERE ARE ALL OUR FRIENDS ? ' " . . . "   150

" ' HAVEN'T TRIED IT ' ". . . . . "   202

" ' IF THEY AIN'T THE CAMP ROBBERS! ' " . . "   232

THE ASSOCIATE HERMITS

CHAPTER I

THE DAWN OF A WEDDING-JOURNEY

MR. AND MRS. HECTOR ARCHIBALD were pros-
perous and happy dwellers in a suburb of one of
our large towns. Fortune had favored them in
many ways—in health and in a good average
happiness. They had reached early middle age,
and their daughter Kate, their only child, had
grown up to be a beautiful and good young
woman, and was on the point of marrying a
young lawyer—Rodney Bringhurst by name—in
every way worthy of her.

Hector Archibald was a little man, with small
bright eyes, and hair slightly touched with gray
and very much inclined to curl. His disposition
was lively. He had a strong liking for cheerful
occurrences, and was always willing to do his
part in the bringing about of such events. Novelty had a charm for him. He was not bound by
precedence and tradition, and if he had found
himself at a dinner which began with coffee and

A   1

ended with oysters on the half-shell, he would have given the unusual meal a most animated consideration, although he might have utterly withheld any subsequent approbation. As a general thing, he revolved in an orbit where one might always be able to find him, were the proper calculations made. But if any one drew a tangent for him, and its direction seemed suitable and interesting, he was perfectly willing to fly off on it.

The disposition of Mrs. Hector Archibald was different. She was born to be guided by customs, fashions, and forms. She believed it was the duty of a married woman to make her home happy, and she did it. But she also believed that in the best domestic circles there were rules and usages for domestic happiness which would apply to every domestic condition and contingency. It frequently troubled her, however, to find that certain customs, forms, or usages of domestic society had changed, and being of a conservative turn of mind, it was difficult for her to adapt herself to these changes. But, thoroughly loyal to the idea that what was done by people she loved and people she respected ought also to be done by her, she earnestly strove to fit herself to new conditions, especially when she saw that by not doing so she would be out of touch with her family and her friends.

Now of course the wedding of their daughter was the only thing in the world that seemed of real importance to Mr. and Mrs. Archibald, and for this all preparations and plans had been agreed upon and made with great good-will and harmony, excepting one thing, and that was the wedding-trip. Strange to say, the young people did not wish to take a wedding-trip. They believed that this old-fashioned custom was unnecessary, troublesome, commonplace, and stupid. In the gardens and grounds of the Archibald mansion, and in the beautiful surrounding country, they had loved each other as lovers, and among these scenes they wished to begin to love each other as a married couple. Why should such distasteful and unpleasant ingredients as railroad-cars, steamboats, and hotels be dashed into the pleasing mixture of their new lives? It · had been arranged that for a year or two, at least, they should live in Kate's dear old home, and why should they not immediately begin that life there?

Mr. Archibald did not favor this plan, and his wife was strongly opposed to it. A wedding without a wedding-trip ought not to be thought of.

" During the honey-moon a young couple should live for each other, with each other, apart from the rest of the world. It is a beautiful custom, which should not be rudely trampled upon," said Mrs. Archibald.

But although Mrs. Archibald cherished a belief that she ought to conform her ideas to the domestic customs of the day, her daughter Kate cherished the belief that the domestic customs of the day ought to conform themselves to her ideas.

"Of course we should like to be alone in the honey-moon," she exclaimed. " We don't object to that; and if there must be a wedding-journey, you and father can take it and we will stay here. Here are servants, books, things to eat, and everything our hearts can desire, and here we would really feel as if we were beginning life as man and wife. As for you two, you both need a vacation, and nothing could be more perfectly appropriate and more delightful to everybody than that you should take our wedding-trip. We don't want it; we will make it a present to you. Take it and be happy, and leave us here to be happy. People have done this sort of thing before, so that it is not absolutely wild and unheard of."

Mr. Archibald welcomed this plan with open arms, and hugged it and his daughter to his breast. It suited him admirably, and he declared that all business and engagements of every kind should be set aside, and that he would be ready to start on the wedding-journey with Mrs. Archibald the moment the ceremony should be completed.

"You will wait until the reception is over, father?" said Kate, laughing.

"Yes," said he, "I will wait for that."

This novel proposition sent a chill through every fibre of Mrs. Archibald's physical organism. At first she did not exactly comprehend it, but when she did, the chills increased. When she had recovered herself a little she began to make objections. This was easy enough, for they crowded into her mind like sheep into a pen; but every objection, as she brought it forth, was ruthlessly set aside or crushed to earth by her

4

daughter or her husband, assisted by her expect-
ant son-in-law, of whom she declared she never
would have believed such a thing had she been
told it.

The discussion ended, of course, by Mrs. Archibald agreeing to go on this absurd wedding-
journey. But the good lady's mental troubles
were not over when she had given her consent.
As this scheme had been devised by those dearest
to her on earth, and as it was certain, these dearest persons assured her, to meet with the approbation of all people of advanced thought—at least
of those whose thought had advanced far enough
to make it worthy of their consideration—she
felt that in doing her part she ought to do it
honestly and with her whole heart; and at her
time of life, to act as a proxy for a young bride
by taking a wedding-journey in that young bride's
place was a very difficult thing for Mrs. Archibald to do honestly and with her whole heart.
But she would try to do it. Whatever else happened, her family must be kept happy, and it
should never be said of her that she hung like a
millstone around the combined neck of that
family when it was unitedly climbing towards altitudes of felicity, which, although she
was not able to discern them, must exist, since
that fact had been so earnestly insisted upon
by Mr. Archibald, Kate, and Rodney Bringhurst.

Thus was this exceptional hymeneal perform-
ance decided upon, and at eleven o'clock on
Wednesday, the 6th of June, the marriage service
was performed. At noon the guests sat down

5

to breakfast, and at two o'clock that afternoon Mr. and Mrs. Hector Archibald departed on the wedding-trip, leaving behind Mr. and Mrs. Bringhurst at home with each other, and "not at home" to the world.

CHAPTER II

AT four o'clock on the afternoon of June 6th Mr.
and Mrs. Hector Archibald arrived at a family
hotel in the capital of their state. Where they
should go from there had not been decided upon.
Nothing in regard to their wedding-journey had
been decided upon except that they were to return to their home on the 6th of July of that
year, and not before. It would have been impossible, with their minds filled with bridal arrangements, for them to make plans for their journey.
But at this first stopping-place, where they were
free from all responsibility and interruptions,
they could, at their leisure, decide where they
should go, how they should go, and what they
should do when they got there.

After the unrest and turmoil of their own home
during the past few weeks, the quiet and repose
of this city hotel were delightful. That evening
they went to the theatre, and after the perform-
ance they had a little supper at a restaurant.

" People may not think we are a newly married
pair," said Mr. Archibald, as he poured out a
glass of wine for his wife, " but it is not impossible that they may see we know how to enjoy ourselves quite as much as if we were."

7

The next morning Mr. Archibald procured a number of railroad maps, time-tables, circulars of steamboat excursions, advertisements of mountain retreats and sea-side resorts, and he and his wife sat down to study these, and to decide upon a destination and a route. After an hour or two of indeterminate examination Mr. Archibald declared himself a little tired, and proposed that they should take a recess from their labors and go and call upon their old friends, the Stanley Dearborns.

"People on wedding-tours do not make calls," said Mrs. Archibald.

"That may be true," said her husband, "in ordinary cases, and although I do not care to announce to everybody the peculiarities of the expedition which we have undertaken, I do not mind in the least telling the Stanley Dearborns all about it. Stanley himself would not appreciate it; he would consider it absurd; but then he is not at home at this time of day, and Mrs. Dearborn is just the woman to enjoy a reform movement of this sort. Besides, she is full of ideas about everything, and she may propose some good place for us to go to."

Mrs. Dearborn was at home, and very glad to see the Archibalds. She was a woman whose soul was in touch with the higher education of women—with female suffrage, the emancipation of the enslaved mind wherever it might be found, and with progress generally. She was a member of many societies, belonged to committees without end, wrote reports and minutes by day and by night, and was one of that ever-increasing class

8

of good people who continually walk forward in order that their weight may help the world to turn over.

In spite of her principles and the advanced position of her thought, Mrs. Dearborn actually leaned back in her chair and laughed heartily when she learned what sort of a journey the Archibalds were taking. In this merriment Mr. Archibald joined with great glee.

"Ever since I left home," he said, "I have wanted to have a chance for a good laugh at this trip we are taking. It is the most delightful joke I have ever known."

Mrs. Archibald could not help smiling, but her brow was clouded. "If this expedition is merely a joke," she said, "I do not think we should have undertaken it; but if it is an earnest assertion of our belief that there should be a change in the customs of society, then I think we should take it seriously, and I see nothing to laugh at."

"My dear Harriet," said Mrs. Dearborn, "we can be good and glad at the same time; and that is what I am, I am sure. What you are doing is the initiation of one of the most worthy reforms of the day, and if it should have an effect in breaking up that wretched custom of the bridal tramp, which is considered so necessary in this country, society should rise up and call you blessed. But it is funny, for all that. I am sure that the first woman who dared to go without crinoline was very funny, and when I heard of a hospital for cats I could not help laughing; but I believed in it, and worked for it. And now where are you going?"

9

"That is what we want to talk to you about," said Mr. Archibald; and for half an hour they talked about it.

At the end of that time it was decided that the mountains were better than the sea or than a quiet lowland nook; and Mrs. Dearborn strongly recommended Sadler's, where she and her husband had spent a part of a summer a few years before.

"We camped out," said she, "and had a fine time. You can camp out at Sadler's more easily and satisfactorily than anywhere else in the world."

Camping suited Mr. Archibald admirably, and, to his surprise, his wife said she might like it very well.

"If people are going to laugh at us," she said, "when they find out we are on a wedding-journey —and they will be sure to find it out in some way or other—I think the fewer people we mingle with the better. I do not think I shall like camping altogether, but I know it is healthful, and I suppose I ought to get used to it. It would be dreadfully lonely for just Mr. Archibald and me, but I suppose we can take some one with us to guide and cook."

"My dear Harriet," said Mrs. Dearborn, "if you are at Sadler's, you can go into any sort of camp you please. I will tell you all about Sadler's. Sadler is a man of progress. His hotel or inn is on the very edge of the forest country, and away from all the centres of resort. He calls his place the terminal link of public travel in that direction. When you leave him you travel privately in any way you like. He has established what he has named a bureau of camping, and he furnishes his patrons with any sort of a camp they may desire. If the party is few in number and of a timid disposition, they can have a camp within shouting distance of his house. If they are brave and adventurous, he will send them out into the depths of the forest. If they like water, he locates them by the shores of a lake. If climbing is their passion, he puts them at the foot of a mountain. Those who want to hunt can do so, and those who dislike fire-arms are placed in a camp where the popping of guns is never heard. He provides tents, guides, provisions, and even dangers and sensations."

" Safety is what I want," interrupted Mrs. Archibald.

" And that he furnishes," said the other, " for those who desire it."

" Sadler is the man for me !" cried Mr. Archibald. " We will go to him, look over his list of camps, and select one to suit us."

" By-the-way," said Mrs. Dearborn, " a thought has struck me. How would you like to take Margery with you ?"

" Margery !" exclaimed Mr. Archibald. " That delightful little girl whom I taught to ride a tricycle when you were visiting us ? I would like it ever so much."

It struck Mrs. Archibald that people on bridal trips did not generally take children or young girls with them, but it also struck her that if they were going into camp it might be pleasant and in many ways advantageous to have some one of her own sex with her; but she had no time to formulate these advantages in her mind before Mrs. Dearborn explained in full.

"Since Mr. Dearborn and I came home from Sadler's," she said, "Margery has been perfectly wild to go there, and as soon as the leaves began to bud in the parks she began to talk about it. We saw no possible chance of her going there, for her father is too busy to leave home for any length of time this season, and I cannot go to the mountains this year, for I must visit my sister, who is not well, and there are three summer conventions that I am obliged to attend. But if you could take her with you, I do not believe she would trouble you in the least, and you would give her great pleasure. Moreover, to speak practically, which I think we always ought to do, it would not be a bad thing on the score of economy, for things are always proportionately cheaper for three people in a camp than for two."

A great many advantages of female companionship now began to creep into Mrs. Archibald's mind: if her husband should take it into his head to go out and hunt at night by the light of a torch; if there should be thunder-storms, and he away with the guide; if he should want to go off and talk to Indians or trappers, and he always did want to go off and talk to people of every class— it would be very pleasant to have even Margery Dearborn with her. So she consented with great good-will to her friend's proposition, and Mrs. Dearborn was much pleased and thankful.

"Margery is a true creature of impulse," she said; "that is really her predominating characteristic, and she will want to bound to the ceiling when she hears she is to go to Sadler's. She is not at home now, but she will be in very soon. You must take luncheon with us."

About a quarter of an hour after that Margery Dearborn came home. She was very glad indeed to see the Archibalds, whom she remembered as the kindest of people ; and when she heard they were going to take her to Sadler's, she gave a scream of delight and threw herself upon Mrs. Archibald's neck.

"You are an angel," she cried, "an angel of blessedness, my dear Aunt Harriet ! Don't you remember, I used to call you that ? Won't you let me call you so still ?" And without waiting for an answer, she rushed to Mr. Archibald, with outstretched hands. " Dear Uncle Archibald, you are just as good as ever, I see. You know, I wouldn't call you Uncle Hector, because hectoring meant scolding, which never had anything to do with you. Sadler's ! Oh, when do we start ?"

" To-morrow is Saturday," replied Mr. Archibald; "we must get together some things we will need for camp-life, and we can start on Monday."

When the visitors were left to themselves for a few moments, Mr. Archibald said to his wife, " Harriet, I am astounded. This girl, who used to ride bareback and jump over fences, is a young lady now, and a handsome one, too. She is quite a different person from the girl I agreed to take with us."

" Mr. Archibald," said his wife, " you never can

remember that in this world people of all ages grow older. She was fourteen when she was visiting us, and that was four years ago, so of course she is a young lady."

"No," he answered, "I don't feel that I am growing any older, and I don't see that you are, and so I totally forget that proclivity in other people. But what do you think now? Can we take this young woman with us to camp? Will she not be a dreadful drag?"

"My dear," said Mrs. Archibald, "I much prefer the young lady to the girl. I don't want to be the only woman in camp, and the nearer the other woman is to my age the better."

"All right," said Mr. Archibald; "if you are satisfied, I am; and, if she will agree to it, we will add our ages for the time being, and divide by three, and then we will all stand on a level."

CHAPTER III

It was in the afternoon of Monday, the 11th of June, when Mr. and Mrs. Archibald, accompanied by Miss Margery Dearborn, arrived at Sadler's, and with feelings of relief alighted from the cramped stage-coach which had brought them eight miles from the railroad station.

"Can this be Sadler's?" said Mr. Archibald, in a tone of surprise.

"Of course it must be," said his wife, "since they brought us here."

"It certainly is the place," said Margery, "for there is the name over that door."

"How do you feel about it?" said Mr. Archibald to his wife.

"I feel very well about it," said she. "Why shouldn't I?"

"How do you feel about it?" he asked of the younger lady.

"Well," she answered, "I don't exactly understand it. I had visions of forests and wilds and tumbling mountain streams and a general air of primevalism, and I am surprised to see this fine hotel with piazzas, and croquet-grounds, and tennis-courts, and gravelled walks, and babies in their carriages, and elderly ladies carrying sun-shades."

15

"But it seems to me that there is a forest behind it," said Mr. Archibald.

"Yes," replied Margery, a little dolefully, "it has that to back it up."

"Don't let us stand here at the bottom of the steps talking," said Mrs. Archibald. "I must say I am very agreeably surprised."

In the wide hall which ran through the middle of the hotel, and not far from the clerk's desk, there sat a large, handsome man, a little past middle age, who, in a hearty voice, greeted the visitors as they entered, but without rising from his chair. This was Peter Sadler, the owner of the hotel, the legal owner of a great deal of the neighboring country, and the actual ruler of more of said country than could be easily marked out upon a map or stated in surveyors' terms.

In fact, Peter Sadler, was king of that portion of the vast district of mountain and forest which could be reached in a day's journey in any direction. If he had wished to extend his domain to points at a greater distance than this he would have done so, but so far he was satisfied with the rights he had asserted. He ruled supreme in that region because he had lived longer in the vicinity than any other white man, because he had a powerful will which did not brook opposition, and because there was no one to oppose him.

On the arable land which lay outside of the forest, and which really belonged to him, there were the houses of the men who farmed his fields, and on the outskirts of the woods were scattered here and there the cabins of the hunt-

16

ers and guides he employed, and these men knew
no law but his will. Of course the laws of the
State covered the district, but such promulga-
tion and enforcement of these as he might consider necessary were generally left to Peter Sadler, and as to his own laws, he was always there
to see that these were observed.

His guests submitted themselves to his will, or
they left his hotel very soon. To people of dis-
cernment and judgment it was not difficult to
submit to the will of this full-bearded, broad-
chested man, who knew so much better than they
did what they ought to do if they wanted to get
all the good out of Sadler's which they were capable of assimilating.

This man, who sat all day in a big rolling-chair,
and who knew everything that was going on in
the hotel, the farm, and the forest about him,
had been a hunter and a guide in his youth, an
Indian-fighter in later years, and when he had
been wounded in both legs, so that it was impossible for him ever to walk again, he came back to
the scenes of his youth and established an inn for
sportsmen — a poor little house at first, which
grew and grew and grew, until it was the large,
well-kept hotel so widely known by his name.

After dinner, at which meal they were waited
upon by women, and not by men in evening-dress
as Margery had begun to fear, Mr. Archibald
sought Peter Sadler and made known to him the
surprise of his party at finding themselves in this
fine hotel.

"What did you expect?" asked Peter, eying
him from head to foot.

"From what we had heard," replied the other, "we supposed we should find some sort of a preparatory camping - ground in the woods, from which we could go out and have a camp of our own."

"That's just what you have found," said Sadler. "In this house you prepare to camp, if you need preparation. If any man, woman, or child comes here and wants to go out to camp, and I see that they are sickly or weak or in any way not fit to live in the woods, I don't let them go one step until they are fit for it. The air and the food and the water they get here will make them fit, if anything will do it, and if these three things don't set them up they simply have to go back where they came from. They can't go into camp from this house. But if they fancy this hotel— and there isn't any reason why anybody shouldn't fancy it—they can stay here as long as they like, and I'll take care of them. Now, sir, if you want to go into camp, the first thing for you to do is to bring your family here and let me take a look at them. I've seen them, of course, but I haven't made up my mind yet whether they are the right sort for camp life. As for you, I think you will do. There isn't much of you, but you look tough."

Mr. Archibald laughed. "That's good rough talk," he said, "and smacks more of camp life than anything I have noticed here. I will go and bring my wife and Miss Dearborn."

"There is another reason why I want to see them," said the bluff Peter. "As you are bent on camping, you'll like to choose a camp, and when

18

anything of that kind is on hand I want to talk to the whole party. I don't care to settle the business with one of them, and then have him come back and say that what has been agreed upon don't suit the others. I want a full meeting or no session."

When Mr. Archibald returned with his wife and Margery, he found Peter Sadler had rolled his chair up to a large circular table at the back of the hall, on which was spread a map of the forest. He greeted the ladies in a loud voice and with a cheery smile.

"And so you want to go camping, do you?" said he. "Sit down and let us talk it over. I think the young lady is all right. She looks spry enough, and I expect she could eat pine-cones like a squirrel if she was hungry and had nothing else. As for you, madam, you don't appear as if anything in particular was the matter with you, and I should think you could stand a Number Three camp well enough, and be all the better for a week or two of it."

"What is a Number Three camp?" asked Margery, before the astonished Mrs. Archibald could speak.

"Well," said Sadler, "it is a camp with a good deal of comfort in it. Our Number One camps are pretty rough. They are for hunters and scientific people. We give them game enough in season, and some bare places where they can make fires and stretch a bit of canvas. That is all they want, to have a truly good time. That is the best camp of all, I think. Number Two camps are generally for fishermen. They always want a chance for pretty good living when they are out in the woods. They stay in camp in the evenings, and like to sit around and have a good time. Number Threes are the best camps we put families into, so you see, madam, I'm rating you pretty high. There's always a log-cabin in these camps, with cots and straw mattresses and plenty of traps for cooking. And, more than that, there is a chance for people who don't tramp or fish to do things, such as walking or boating, according to circumstances. There's one of our camps has a croquet-ground."

"Oh, we don't want that !" cried Margery, "it would simply ruin every illusion that is left to me."

"Glad to hear that," said Peter. "If you want to play croquet, stay at the hotel; that's what I say. Now, then, here are the camps, and there's plenty of them to choose from. You've come in a good time, for the season isn't fairly begun yet. Next month every camp will be full, with the hotel crowded with people waiting for their turns."

"What we want," said Margery, rising and looking over the map, "is the wildest Number Three you have."

"Oh, ho !" said Peter. "Not so fast, miss ; perhaps we'll wait and see what this lady has to say first. If I'm not mistaken, madam, I think you're inclined the other way, and I don't put people into camps that they will be wanting to leave after the first rainy day. Now let me show you what I've got. Here is one, four hours' walk, horses for women, with a rocky stream through the middle of it,"

"That is grand!" cried Margery. "Is it really in the woods?"

"Now let me do the talking," said Peter. "They are all in the woods; we don't make camps in pasture-fields. Even the Number Sevens, where the meals are sent to the campers from the hotel, and they have bath-tubs, are in the woods. Now here is another one, about three miles west from the one I just showed you, but the same distance from here. This, you see, is on the shore of a lake, with fishing, boating, and bathing, if you can stand cold water."

"Glorious!" cried Margery. "That is exactly what we want. A lake will be simply heavenly!"

"Everything seems to suit you, miss," said Peter, "just as soon as you hear of it. But suppose we consider more of them before you choose. Some two miles north of here, in the thickest of the forest, in a clearing that I made, there is a small camp that strikes the fancy of some people. There is a little stream there and it has fish in it too, and it runs through one corner of the log-cabin, so there are seven or eight feet of the stream inside the house, and on rainy days you can sit there and fish; and some people like to go to sleep with the running water gurgling close to them where they can hear it when they are in bed. Then there's an owl to this camp. The men heard him there when they were making the clearing, and he's never left the spot. Some people who were out there said they never felt as much away from the world as they did listening to that little stream gurgling and that owl hooting."

"I believe," exclaimed Margery, "that in a place like that I could write poetry !"

"It would give me the rheumatism and the blues," said Mrs. Archibald, upon which Peter Sadler exclaimed,

"That settles that. Now then, here is another."

Several other camps were considered, but it was the general conclusion that the one by the lake was the most desirable. It had a good cabin with three rooms, with plenty of open space, near by, for the tents of the guides ; there was a boat which belonged to the camp, and in every way it seemed so suitable that Mr. Archibald secured it. He thought the price was rather high, but as it included guides, provisions, fishing-tackle, and in fact everything needed, he considered that although it might cost as much as lodgings in a city hotel, they would get more good out of it.

" Has this camp any name?" asked the enthusiastic Margery, in the course of the conference.

"That's about your twenty-seventh question, miss," said Peter, "but it's one I can answer. Yes, it's got a name. It's called Camp Rob."

" Oh !" ejaculated Margery, in a disappointed tone. "What a name !"

" Yes," said Peter, "it isn't much of a name. The first people who went out there named it that, and it stuck to it, and it's all it's got. Camps are like horses — we've got to tell them apart, and so we give them names, and that's Camp Rob."

CHAPTER IV

A CATARACT OF INFORMATION

PETER SADLER would have been glad to have the Archibald party stay at his hotel for a few days, and Mrs. Archibald would have been perfectly satisfied to remain there until they were ready to return to their own house, but her husband and Margery were impatient to be in the woods, and it was therefore decided to start for the camp the next day. Peter Sadler was a man of system, and his arrangements were made promptly and rapidly.

"You've got to have a guide," said he, "and another man to help him, and I think I'll give you Phil Matlack. Phil is an old hand at the business, and if you don't know what you want, he'll tell you. If you are in Phil's hands, you needn't be afraid anything will happen to you. Whatever you want, ask him for it, and ten to one he'll have it, whether it's information or fish-hooks. I tell you again, you're lucky to be here early and get the best of everything. Camp Rob with Phil Matlack will stand at a premium in three or four weeks from now."

That evening after supper Mr. Archibald lighted a cigar and went out into the grounds in front of the hotel, where he was presently joined by his wife.

"Where is Margery?" asked he.

"She is in her room," replied Mrs. Archibald, "but she called to me that she would be down directly."

In about ten minutes down came Margery and floated out upon the lawn. She was dressed in white, with flowers in her hair, and she was more charming, Mr. Archibald said, as she approached, than even the sunset sky.

"You should not speak in that way of works of nature," said his wife.

"Isn't she a work of nature?" he asked.

"Not altogether," was the wise reply. "Why did you dress yourself in that fashion?" she asked Margery. "I did not suppose you would bring such a fine gown, as we started out to go into camp. And even in this hotel a travelling-suit is good enough for any one."

"Oh, I tucked this into one of my bags," replied Margery. "I always like to have something nice to fall back upon. Don't you want to take a little stroll, Aunt Harriet?"

Mr. Archibald leaned back in his garden-chair and slowly puffed his cigar, and as he puffed he took his eyes from the sunset sky and watched his wife and Margery.

A little beyond them, as they walked, sat two elderly ladies on a bench, wearing shawls, and near by stood a girl in a short dress, with no hat on, and a long plait down her back. A little farther on was a tennis-court, and four people, apparently young, were playing tennis. There were two men, and neither of them wore a tennis-suit. One was attired as a bicyclist, and the other

wore ordinary summer clothes. The young wom-
en were dressed in dark-blue flannel and little
round hats, which suggested to Mr. Archibald
the deck of a yacht.

Near the hotel was an elderly gentleman walking up and down by himself, and on the piazza
were the rest of the guests he had seen at the
table; not very many of them, for it was early in
the season.

Mr. Archibald now turned his eyes again to the
sky. It was still beautiful, although its colors
were fading, and after a time he looked back
towards his wife. She was now talking to the
two elderly ladies on the bench, and Margery was
engaged in conversation with the girl with the
plait down her back.

"When I finish my cigar," thought Mr. Archibald, "I will go myself and take a stroll." And
it struck him that he might talk to the old gentleman, who was still walking up and down in
front of the hotel. After contemplating the tops
of some forest trees against the greenish-yellow
of the middle sky, he turned his eyes again towards his wife, and found that the two elderly
ladies had made room for her on the bench, that
the tennis-game had ceased, and that one of the
girls in blue flannel had joined this group and
was talking to Margery.

In a few moments all the ladies on the bench
rose, and Mrs. Archibald and one of them walked
slowly towards an opening in the woods. The
other lady followed with the little girl, and Margery and the young woman in blue walked in the
same direction, but not in company with the rest

of the party. The two young men, with the other tennis-player between them, walked over from the tennis-court and joined the first group, and they all stopped just as they reached the woods. There they stood and began talking to each other, after which one of the young men and the young woman approached a large tree, and he poked with a stick into what was probably a hole near its roots, and Mr. Archibald supposed that the discussion concerned a snake-hole or a hornets' nest. Then Margery and the other young woman came up, and they looked at the hole. Now the whole company walked into the woods and disappeared. In about ten minutes Mr. Archibald finished his cigar and was thinking of following his wife and Margery, when the two elderly ladies and Mrs. Archibald came out into the open and walked towards the hotel. Then came the little girl, running very fast as she passed the tree with the hole near its roots. In a few minutes Mrs. Archibald stopped and looked back towards the woods ; then she walked a little way in that direction, leaving her companions to go to the hotel. Now the young man in the bicycle suit emerged from the woods, with a girl in dark-blue flannel on each side of him.

"Upon my word !" exclaimed Mr. Archibald, and rising to his feet, advanced towards his wife ; but before he reached her, Margery emerged from the wood road, escorted by the young man in the summer suit.

"Upon my word," Mr. Archibald remarked, this time to his wife, "that ward of ours is not given to wasting time."

" It seems so, truly," said she, " and I think her
mother was right when she called her a creature
of impulse. Let us wait here until they come
up. We must all go in ; it is getting chilly."

In a few minutes Margery and the young man
had reached them.

"Thank you very much," said this creature of
impulse to her escort. " My uncle and aunt will
take care of me now. Aunt Harriet and Uncle
Archibald, this is Mr. Clyde. He saw a great
snake go into a hole over there just before supper-time, and I think we ought all to be very
careful how we pass that way."

" I don't think there is very much danger after
nightfall," said Mr. Clyde, who was a pleasant
youth with brown hair, "and to-morrow I'll see
if I can kill him. It's a bad place for a snake
to have a hole, just where ladies would be apt to
take their walks."

" I don't think the snake will trouble us much,"
said Mrs. Archibald, "for we leave to-morrow.
Still, it would be a good thing to kill it."

After this there were a few remarks made
about snakes, and then Mr. Clyde bade them
good-evening.

" How in the world, Margery," said Mrs. Archibald, " did you get acquainted so quickly with
that young man—and who is he ?"

" Oh, it all happened quite naturally," said she.
" As we turned to go out of the woods he was the
gentleman nearest to me, and so of course he
came with me. Those two girls are sisters, and
their name is Dodworth. They introduced Mr.
Clyde and the other gentleman, Mr Raybold, to

me. But that was after you had been talking to Mrs. Dodworth, their mother, who is Mr. Raybold's aunt. The other lady, with the shawl on, is Mrs. Henderson, and—would you believe it?— she's grandmother to that girl in the short dress! She doesn't begin to look old enough. The Dodworths don't go into camp at all, but expect to stay here for two weeks longer, and then they go to the sea-shore. Mrs. Henderson leaves day after to-morrow.

"Mr. Clyde and his friend live in Boston. They are both just beginning to practise law, though Mr. Clyde says that Mr. Raybold would rather be an actor, but his family objects. The old gentleman who is walking up and down in front of the hotel has heart-disease, some people say—but that is not certain. He stayed here all last summer, and perhaps he will this year. In two weeks hardly any of the people now in this hotel will be here. One family is going into camp when the father and two sons come on to join them, and the rest are going to the sea-shore, except one lady. You may have noticed her— the one with a dark-purple dress and a little purple cap. She's a school-teacher, and she will spend the rest of the summer with her sister in Pennsylvania.

"That man Phil Matlack, who is going with us to-morrow, is quite a character, and I expect I shall like him awfully. They say that about five years ago he killed a man who made an attack on him in the woods, but he was never tried for it, nor was anything whatever done to him, because Mr. Sadler said he was right, and he would not have any nonsense about it. There are people about here who believe that Phil Matlack would fight a bear single-handed if it happened to be necessary. Mr. Sadler would do it himself if he could walk. Nobody knows how many men he killed when he was fighting Indians; and, would you believe it? his wife is a plain, little, quiet woman, who lives in some part of the hotel where nobody ever sees her, because she is rather bashful and dislikes company.

"The other person who is going with us is not very much more than a boy, though they say he is very strong and a good hunter. His name is Martin Sanders, and I forgot to say that the old gentleman with the heart-disease is named Parker.

"It's generally thought that Phil Matlack would rather have some one else than Martin Sanders to go with him, because he says Martin knows too much. The fact is that Martin is well educated, and could have gone into some good business, but he was so fond of the woods that he gave up everything to come out here and learn guiding. You know we were told that our camp in the woods has three rooms in it? Well, it really has four, for there was an artist there last year who built a little room for a studio for rainy days. I expect Mr. Sadler forgot that, or didn't think it worth counting. There are no snakes at all where we are going to camp, but two miles farther on there are lots of them."

"Over the brink of Niagara," interjected Mr. Archibald, "they say eighteen million cubic feet of water pour every minute. Where on earth,

29

Margery, did you fill your mind with all that information?"

" I got it from those two Dodworth girls and Mr. Clyde," said she. " Mr. Raybold told me some things, too, but mostly about his bicycle. He feels badly about it, because he brought it here, and now he finds there is no place to use it. I should think he ought to have known that the primeval forest isn't any place for a bicycle."

" Mr. Archibald," said Mrs. Archibald, when they had retired to their room, " I did not agree with you when you wished we could have started for camp to-day, but now I am quite of your mind."

Tuesday was fine, and preparations were made for the Archibald party to start for their camp after an early luncheon.

The bluff and hearty Peter took such an interest in everything that was being done for their comfort, giving special heed to all the possible requirements of Mrs. Archibald, that the heart of Mr. Archibald was touched.

" I wish," said he to his good-natured host, " that you were going with us. I do not know any one I would rather camp with than you."

" If I could do it," replied Peter, " I'd like it ever so well. So far as I have been able to make you out, you are the sort of a man I'd be willing to run a camp for. What I like about you is that you haven't any mind of your own. There is nothing I hate worse than to run against a man with a mind of his own. Of course there have to be such fellows, but let them keep away from me. There is no room here for more than one mind, and I have pre-empted the whole section."

Mr. Archibald laughed. "Your opinion of me does not sound very complimentary," he said.

"It is complimentary!" roared Peter Sadler, striking the table with his fist. "Why, I tell you, sir, I couldn't say anything more commendable of you if I tried! It shows that you are a man of common-sense, and that's pretty high praise. Everything I've told you to do you've done. Everything I've proposed you've agreed to. You see for yourself that I know what is better for you and your party than you do, and you stand up like a man and say so. Yes, sir; if a rolling-chair wasn't as bad for the woods as the bicycle that Boston chap brought down here, I'd go along with you."

Mr. Archibald had a very sharp sense of the humorous, and in his enjoyment of a comical situation he liked company. His heart was stirred to put his expedition in its true light before this man who was so honest and plain-spoken. "Mr. Sadler," said he, "if you will take it as a piece of confidential information, and not intended for the general ear, I will tell you what sort of a holiday my wife and I are taking. We are on a wedding-journey." And then he told the story of the proxy bridal tour.

Peter Sadler threw himself back in his chair and laughed with such great roars that two hunting-dogs, who were asleep in the hall, sprang to their feet and dashed out of the back door, their tails between their legs. -

"By the Lord Harry!" cried Peter Sadler, "you and your wife are a pair of giants. I don't say anything about that young woman, for I

31

don't believe it would have made any difference
to her whether you were on a wedding-trip or
travelling into the woods to bury a child. I tell
you, sir, you mayn't have a mind that can give
out much, but you've got a mind that can take in
the biggest kind of thing, and that is what I call
grand. It is the difference between a canyon and
a mountain. There are lots of good mountains
in this world, and mighty few good canyons.
Tom, you Tom, come here !"

In answer to the loud call a boy came running up.

"Go into my room," said Peter Sadler, "and
bring out a barrel bottle, large size, and one of
the stone jars with a red seal on it. Now, sir,"
said he to Mr. Archibald, "I am going to give you
a bottle of the very best whiskey that ever a
human being took into the woods, and a jar of
smoking-tobacco a great deal too good for any
king on any throne. They belong to my private
stock, and I am proud to make them a present to
a man who will take a wedding-trip to save his
grown-up daughter the trouble. As for your wife,
there'll be a basket that will go to her with my
compliments, that will show her what I think of
her. By-the-way, sir, have you met Phil Matlack ?"

"No, I have not !" exclaimed Mr. Archibald,
with animation. "I have heard something about
him, and before we start I should like to see the
man who is going to take charge of us in camp."

"Well, there he is, just passing the back door.
Hello, Phil ! come in here."

When the eminent guide, Phil Matlack, entered

the hall, Mr. Archibald looked at him with some
surprise, for he was not the conventional tall,
gaunt, wiry, keen-eyed backwoodsman who had
naturally appeared to his mental vision. This
man was of medium height, a little round-shoul-
dered, dressed in a gray shirt, faded brown trousers very baggy at the knees, a pair of conspicuous
blue woollen socks, and slippers made of carpet.
His short beard and his hair were touched with
gray, and he wore a small jockey cap. With the
exception of his eyes, Mr. Matlack's facial features were large, and the expression upon them
was that of a mild and generally good-natured
tolerance of the world and all that is in it. It
may be stated that this expression, combined with
his manner, indicated also a desire on his part
that the world and all that is in it should tolerate
him. Mr. Archibald's first impressions of the
man did not formulate themselves in these terms;
he simply thought that the guide was a slipshod
sort of a fellow.

" Phil," said Mr. Sadler, " here is the gentleman
you are going to take into camp."

" Glad to see him," said Matlack; "hope he'll
like it."

" And I want to say to you, Phil," continued Sadler," right before him, that he is a first-class man
for you to have in charge. I don't believe you
ever had a better one. He's a city man, and it's
my opinion he don't know one thing about hunting, fishing, making a camp-fire, or even digging
bait. I don't suppose he ever spent a night outside of a house, and doesn't know any more about
the weather than he does about planting cab-

bages. He's just clean, bright, and empty, like a new peach-basket. What you tell him he'll know, and what you ask him to do he'll do, and if you want a better man than that to take into camp, you want too much. That's all I've got to say."

Matlack looked at Peter Sadler and then at Mr. Archibald, who was leaning back in his chair, his bright eyes twinkling.

"How did you find out all that about him?" he asked.

"Humph!" exclaimed Peter Sadler. "Don't you suppose I can read a man's character when I've had a good chance at him? Now how about the stores—have they all gone on?"

"They were sent out early this mornin'," said Matlack, "and we can start as soon as the folks are ready."

CHAPTER V

CAMP ROB

It was early in the afternoon when the Archibald party took up the line of march for Camp
Rob. The two ladies, supplied by Mrs. Sadler
with coarse riding-skirts, sat each upon a farm-
horse, and Mr. Archibald held the bridle of the
one that carried his wife. Matlack and Martin
Sanders, the young man who was to assist him,
led the way, while a led horse, loaded with the
personal baggage of the travellers, brought up
the rear.

Their way wound through a forest over a wood
road, very rough and barely wide enough for the
passage of a cart. The road was solemn and
still, except where, here and there, an open space
allowed the sunlight to play upon a few scattered
wild flowers and brighten the sombre tints of the
undergrowth.

After a ride which seemed a long one to the
ladies, who wished they had attired themselves in
walking-costume, the road and the forest suddenly
came to an end, and before them stretched out
the waters of a small lake. Camp Rob was not
far from the head of the lake, and for some distance above and below the forest stood back from
the water's edge. In the shade of a great oak-

35

tree there stood a small log-house, rude enough to look at, but moderately comfortable within, and from this house to the shore a wide space was cleared of bushes and undergrowth.

The lake was narrow in proportion to its length, which was about two miles, and on the other side the forest looked like a solid wall of green reflected in the water beneath. Even Mrs. Archibald, whose aching back began to have an effect upon her disposition, was delighted with the beauty of the scene, which delight endured until she had descended from her horse and entered the log-cabin in which she was to dwell for a time.

It is not necessary to describe the house, nor is it necessary to dive into the depths of Mrs. Archibald's mind as she gazed about her, passing silently from room to room of the little house. She was a good woman, and she had made up her mind that she would not be a millstone around the necks of her companions. Many people have been happy in camps, and, indeed, camp-life has become one of the features of our higher civilization, and this, from what she had heard, must be a camp above the common. So, think what she might, she determined to make no open complaint. If it were possible for her to be happy here, she would be happy.

As for Margery, no determination was needed in her case. Everything was better than she had expected to find it. The cabin, with the bark on almost everything, even the furniture, was just what a house in the woods ought to be; and when she entered the little studio, which was nearer allied to the original forest than any other part of the house, she declared that that must be her room, and that living there she would feel almost like a dryad in an oak.

"You've camped out before?" said Phil Matlack to Mr. Archibald, as he was taking a survey of the scene.

"Oh yes," said the other, "I've been out a few days at a time with fishing-parties, but we never had such a fine camp as this—so well located and such good accommodations."

"You are a fisherman, then?" said the guide.

"Yes. I am very fond of it. I've fished ever since I was a boy, and know a good deal about bait, in spite of what Mr. Sadler said."

"I had an idea of that sort," remarked Phil, "but it ain't no use to contradict Peter. It helps keep up his spirits for him to think he can read the characters of people just as quick as he can aim a rifle. And it's a mighty important thing to keep Peter's spirits up. If Peter's spirits was to go down, things round here would flatten out worse than a rotten punkin when it's dropped."

It did not take long to establish the new-comers in their woodland quarters. The tent for the two men, which had arrived in the morning, was pitched not far from the cabin, and then Matlack and Martin went to work to prepare supper. The dining-room in pleasant weather was the small space in front of the house, where there was a table made of a wide board supported by stakes, with a low and narrow board on each side, also resting on stakes, and forming seats.

The supper was a better one and better served

than any of the party had expected. The camp outfit included table-cloths, and even napkins.

"To-morrow," said Matlack, as he brought a dish of hot and savory broiled ham, "after Mr. Archibald gets to work, we'll have some fish."

Mrs. Archibald had been a little fearful that under these primitive conditions the two men might expect to sit at the table with them, but she need have had no such fears. Matlack and Martin cooked and waited with a skill and deftness which would have surprised any one who did not reflect that this was as much their business as hunting or woodcraft.

After supper a camp-fire was built at a safe distance from the house, for although the evening air was but slightly cool, a camp without a camp-fire would not be a camp. The party ranged themselves around it, Mrs. Archibald on a rug brought from the cabin, and her husband and Margery on the ground. Mr. Archibald lighted his pipe, the fire lighted the trees and the lake, and joy inexpressible lighted the heart of Margery.

"If I could smoke a pipe," said she, "and get Mr. Matlack to come here and tell me how he killed a man, I should be perfectly happy."

That night Mrs. Archibald lay awake on her straw mattress. Absolute darkness was about her, but through the open window she could see, over the tops of the trees on the other side of the lake, one little star.

"If I could get any comfort out of that little star," thought the good lady, "I would do it; but I can't do it, and there is nothing else to comfort me."

On the other side of the room, on another straw
mattress, she could hear her husband breathing
steadily. Then, upon the bare boards of the floor,
which were but a few inches below her little cot-
bed, she thought she heard the patter of small
feet. A squirrel, perhaps, or, horrible to think
of, it might be a rat. She was sure rats would
eat straw beds, and her first impulse was to wake
Mr. Archibald ; but she hesitated, he was sleeping so soundly. Still she listened, and now she
became almost certain that what she heard was
not the patter of small feet ; it sounded more like
something soft which was dragging itself over the
floor — possibly a snake. This idea was simply
awful, and she sat up in bed. Still she did not
call Mr. Archibald, for should he suddenly spring
on the floor, he would be in more danger from the
snake than she was.

She listened and she listened, but she heard
nothing more, and then her reason began to assure her that a snake's movements on a bare floor
would be absolutely noiseless ; but in a moment
all thoughts of serpents were driven from her
head. Outside of the cabin she heard a sound
that could be nothing less than the footsteps of
some living creature — a wild beast, perhaps a
panther. The door was shut and fastened, but
the window was open. To call Mr. Archibald and
tell him a wild beast was walking outside the
house would be positively wicked. Half-awak-
ened, he would probably rush out of the door to
see what it was. What could she do ? For an
instant she thought of lighting a candle and
standing it in the window. She knew that wild

beasts were afraid of fire, and she did not believe that even a panther would dare jump over a lighted candle. But if she struck a match and got up, she would waken her husband ; and, besides, if the wind, of which she could feel a puff every now and then, did not blow out the candle, it might blow it over and set fire to the cabin.

She heard the footsteps no more, and lay down again, but not to sleep. The wind seemed to be rising, and made a wild, unearthly sound as it surged through the trees which surrounded and imprisoned her, and shut her out from the world in which she was born and in which she ought to live. There was a far-away sound which came to her ears once, twice, thrice, and which might have been the call of some ghostly bird or the war-whoop of an Indian. At last she drew the covering over her head, determined that, so long as she could not see, she would not hear.

"A wedding-journey !" she said to herself, and the idea, coupled with the sense of her present grewsome and doleful condition, was so truly absurd and ridiculous that she could not restrain a melancholy laugh.

"What is the matter, my dear ?" exclaimed Mr. Archibald, suddenly turning over in his bed. "Are you choking? Is the room too close? Shall I open the door ?"

"No, indeed," she said, "for that was a laugh you heard. I couldn't help laughing at the thought that there should be two such idiots in the world as you and myself."

"It is idiotic, isn't it ?" said Mr. Archibald. "It is gloriously idiotic, and it will do us both a world of good. It is such a complete and perfect change that I don't wonder you laugh." Then he laughed himself, clearly and loudly, and turned over on his side and went to sleep.

Mrs. Archibald felt certain that she would not sleep another wink that night, but she did sleep seven hours and a half, and was awakened by Margery singing outside her window.

CHAPTER VI

No thoughts of idiocy crossed the minds of any of the camping party during their first breakfast under the great oak-tree. The air, the sunlight, the rippling waters of the lake, the white clouds in the blue sky, the great trunks of the trees, the rustling of the leaves, the songs of the birds, the hum of insects, the brightness of everything, their wonderful appetites—the sense of all these things more than filled their minds.

For the greater part of that day Mr. Archibald fished, sometimes in a stream which ran into the head of the lake about a quarter of a mile above the camp, and sometimes on the shores of the lake itself. Margery sketched ; her night in the studio had filled her with dreams of art, and she had discovered in a corner a portable easel made of hickory sticks with the bark on, and she had tucked some drawing materials into one of her bags.

Mrs. Archibald was a little tired with her journey of the day before, and contented herself with sitting in the shade in pleasant places, occupied with some needle-work she had brought with her, and trying to discipline her mind to habits of happiness in camp. This was not very difficult during the first part of this beautiful day,

but towards the end of the afternoon she began
to think less of the joys of a free life in the heart
. of nature and more of the pleasure of putting on
her bonnet and going out to make some calls
upon her friends. In this state of mind it pleased
her to see Phil Matlack coming towards her.

"Would you like a cup of tea, ma'am?" said he.

"No, thank you," she answered. "It would
seem rather odd to have afternoon tea in the
woods, and I really don't care for it."

"We can have 'most anything in the woods,
ma'am," said Matlack, "that we can have anywhere else, providin' you don't mind what sort
of fashion you have it in. I thought it might be
sort of comfortin' to you to have a cup of tea.
I've noticed that in most campin' parties of the
family order there's generally one or two of them
that's lonesome the first day; and the fact is I
don't count on anything particular bein' done on
the first day in camp, except when the party is
regular hunters or fishermen. It's just as well
for some of them to sit round on the first day and
let things soak into them, provided it isn't rain,
and the next day they will have a more natural
feelin' about what they really want to do. Now
I expect you will be off on some sort of a tramp
to-morrow, ma'am, or else be out in the boat; and
as for that young lady, she's not goin' to sketch
no more after to-day. She's got young Martin
out in the boat, restin' on his oars, while she's put-
tin' him into her picture. She's rubbed him out
so often that I expect he'll fall asleep and tumble
overboard, or else drop one of his oars."

"Mr. Matlack," said Mrs. Archibald, "will you

please sit down a moment? I want to ask you something."

"Certainly, ma'am," said he, and forthwith seated himself on a log near by, picking up a stick as he did so, and beginning to shave the bark from it with his pocket-knife.

"Do you know," said she, "if there are panthers in these woods?"

Matlack looked up at her quickly. "I expect you heard them walkin' about your cabin last night," said he; "and not only panthers, but most likely a bear or two, and snakes rustlin' in the leaves; and, for all I know, coons or 'possums climbin' in and out of the window."

"Oh, nothing so bad as that," she replied. "I only thought—"

"Excuse me, ma'am," he interrupted. "I didn't mean that you heard all those things, but most likely a part of them. Hardly any family parties goes into camp that some of them don't hear wild beasts the first night. But they never come no more. Them kind of wild beasts I call first-nighters, and they're about the worst kind we've got, because they really do hurt people by scratchin' and clawin' at their nerves, whereas the real wild beasts in these parts—and they're mighty scarce, and never come near camp—don't hurt nobody."

"I am glad to hear it," said she. "But what on earth can be keeping Mr. Archibald? When he started out after dinner he said he would be back very soon."

"Oh, he's got the fever, ma'am," said Matlack.

"Fever!" exclaimed Mrs. Archibald, dropping her work in her lap.

44

"Oh, don't be frightened," said he ; "it is only the fishin' fever. It don't hurt anybody ; it only keeps the meals waitin'. You see, we are pretty nigh the first people out this year, and the fish bite lively. Are you fond of fishin', ma'am ?"

"No, indeed," said she ; "I dislike it. I think it is cruel and slimy and generally unpleasant."

"I expect you'll spend most of your time in the boat," suggested Matlack. "Your husband rows, don't he ?"

"He doesn't row me," said Mrs. Archibald, with earnestness. "I never go out in a boat except with a regular boatman. I suppose you have a larger boat than the one that young man is in ? I can see it from here, and it looks very small."

"No, ma'am," said Matlack; "that's the only one we've got. And now I guess I'll go see about supper. This has been a lazy day for us, but we always do calc'late on a lazy day to begin with."

"It strikes me," said Matlack to himself, as he walked away, "that this here camp will come to an end pretty soon. The man and the young woman could stand it for a couple of weeks, but there's nothing here for the old lady, and it can't be long before she'll have us all out of the woods again."

"You can come in," called Margery, about ten minutes after this conversation ; and young Martin, who had not the least idea of going to sleep in the boat, dipped his oars in the water and rowed ashore, pulled the boat up on the beach, and then advanced to the spot where

Margery was preparing to put away her drawing materials.

"Would you mind letting me see your sketch?" said he.

"Oh no," said she; "but you'll see it isn't very much like the scene itself. When I make a drawing from nature I never copy everything I see just as if I were making a photograph. I suppose you think I ought to draw the boat just as it is, but I always put something of my own in my pictures. And that, you see, is a different kind of a boat from the one you were in. It is something like Venetian boats."

"It isn't like anything in this part of the world, that is true," said the young man, as he held the drawing in his hand; "and if it had been more like a gondola it would not have suited the scene. I think you have caught the spirit of the landscape very well; but if you don't object to a little criticism, I should say that the shore over there is too near the foreground. It seems to me that the picture wants atmosphere; that would help the distance very much."

"Do you draw?" asked Margery, in surprise.

"I used to be very fond of sketching," said he. "I stayed at Sadler's a good part of the last winter, and when I wasn't out hunting I made a good many drawings of winter scenes. I would be glad to show them to you when we go back."

"Well," said she, "if I had known you were an artist I would not have asked you to go out there and sit as a model."

"Oh, I am not an artist," replied Martin; "I only draw, that's all. But if you make any more

46

water sketches and would like me to put some ducks or any other kind of wild-fowl in the foreground I will be glad to do it for you. I have made a specialty of natural-history drawings. Don't bother yourself about that easel; I'll carry up your things for you."

About half-way to the cabin Margery suddenly stopped and turned round towards the young man, who was following her. "How did you come to be a guide?" she asked.

He smiled. "That's because I was born a naturalist and a sportsman. I went into business when I finished my education, but I couldn't stand that, and as I couldn't afford to become a gentleman sportsman, I came here as a guide. I'm getting a lot of experience in this sort of life, and when I've saved money enough I'm going on an exploring expedition, most likely to Central America. That's the kind of life that will suit me."

" And write a book about it?" asked Margery.

" Most likely," said he.

That night, after supper, Margery remarked : " Our two guides are American citizens, and I don't see why they can't eat at the table with us instead of waiting until we have finished. We are all free and equal in the woods."

" Margery Dearborn !" exclaimed Mrs. Archibald. " What are you talking about?"

She was going to say that if there were one straw more needed to break her back, that straw would be the sight of the two guides sitting at the table with them, but she restrained herself. She did not want Mr. Archibald to know anything about the condition of her back.

"So long as they don't want to do it, and don't do it," said she, "pray don't let us say anything about it. Let's try to make things as pleasant as we can."

Mr. Archibald was lighting his pipe, and when he was sure the tobacco was sufficiently ignited he took the pipe from his mouth and turned towards his wife.

"Harriet," said he, "you have been too much alone to-day. I don't know what I shall do to-morrow; but whatever it is, I am going to take you with me."

"Of course that depends on what it is you do," she answered. "But I will try to do everything I can."

Mr. Archibald heaved a little sigh, which was not noticed by any one, because it sounded like a puff.

"I am afraid," he thought, "that this camping business is not going to last very much longer, and we shall be obliged to make the rest of our wedding-journey in a different style."

The next morning, when Mr. Archibald went out of his cabin door, he looked over the lake and saw a bird suddenly swoop down upon the water, breaking the smooth surface into sparkles of silver, and then rise again, a little silvery fish glittering in its claws.

"Beautifully done!" said he. "A splendid stroke!" And then turning, he looked up the lake, and not far from the water's edge he saw Margery walking with Mr. Clyde, while Mr. Raybold followed a little in the rear.

"Harriet," he cried, quickly stepping into the

48

cabin again, " look out here ! What is the meaning of this ?"

Mrs. Archibald was dressed, and came out.
When she saw the trio approaching them, she
was not so much surprised as was her husband.

"I don't know the meaning of anything that
happens in these woods," she said ; " but if a lot
of people have come from the hotel with those
young men I cannot say I am sorry."

" Come," said her husband, " we must look into
this."

In two minutes the Archibalds had met the
new - comers, who advanced with outstretched
hands, as if they had been old friends. Mr. Archibald, not without some mental disquietude at
this intrusion upon the woodland privacy of his
party, was about to begin a series of questions,
when he was forestalled by Margery.

"Oh, Uncle Archibald and Aunt Harriet !" she
exclaimed, "Mr. Clyde and Mr. Raybold have
come out here to camp. Their camp is right
next to ours, and it is called Camp Roy. You
see, some years ago there was a large camping
party came here, and they called the place Camp
Rob Roy, but it was afterwards divided, and one
part called Camp Rob and the other Camp Roy."

"Indeed !" interrupted Mr. Archibald. "Mr.
Sadler did not tell us that ours was only half a
camp with only half a name."

"I don't suppose he thought of it," said Margery. "And the line between the two camps
is just three hundred feet above our cabin. I
don't suppose anybody ever measures it off, but
there it is; and Mr. Clyde and Mr. Raybold have

D   49

taken Camp Roy, which hasn't any house on it. They started before daybreak this morning, and brought a tent along with them, which they have pitched just back of that little peninsula ; and they haven't any guide, because they want to attend to their own cooking and everything, and the man who brought the tent and other things has gone back. They are going to live there just like real backwoodsmen, and they have a boat of their own, which is to be brought up from the bottom of the lake somewhere—I mean from the lower end of the lake. And, Aunt Harriet, may I speak to you a moment ?"

With this the young woman drew Mrs. Archibald aside, and in a low voice asked if she thought it would be out of the way to invite the two young men to take breakfast with them, as it was not likely they had all their cooking things in order so early.

Five people sat down to breakfast under the great oak-tree, and it was a lively meal. Mr. Archibald's mental disquiet, in which were now apparent some elements of resentment, had not subsided, but the state of his mind did not show itself in his demeanor, and he could not help feeling pleased to see that his wife was in better spirits. He had always known that she liked company.

After breakfast he took Matlack aside. "I don't understand this business," said he. "When I hired this camp I supposed we were to have it to ourselves ; but if there are other camps jammed close against it we may be in the midst of a great public picnic before a week is out."

"Oh, that camp over there isn't much of a camp," replied the guide. "The fact is, it is only the tail end of a camp, and I don't suppose Peter Sadler thought anybody would be likely to take it just now, and so didn't think it worth while to speak of it. Of course it's jammed up against this one, as you say; but then the people in one camp haven't the right to cross the line into another camp if the people in the other camp don't want them to."

"Line!" said Mr. Archibald. "It is absurd to think of lines in a place like this. And I have no intention of making myself disagreeable by ordering people off my premises. But I would like to know if there is another camp three hundred feet on this side of our cabin, or three hundred feet back of it."

"No, sir," said Matlack, speaking promptly; "there isn't another camp between this and the lower end of the lake. There's a big one there, and it's taken; but the people aren't coming until next month."

"If a larger party had taken Camp Roy," said Mr. Archibald to his wife a little later, "I should not mind it so much. But two young men! I do not like it."

CHAPTER VII

It was at the close of a pleasant afternoon four days after the arrival of the young men at Camp Roy, and Mrs. Archibald was seated on a camp-stool near the edge of the lake intently fishing. By her side stood Phil Matlack, who had volunteered to interpose himself between her and all the disagreeable adjuncts of angling. He put the bait upon her hook, he told her when her cork was bobbing sufficiently to justify a jerk, and when she caught a little fish he took it off the hook. Fishing in this pleasant wise had become very agreeable to the good lady, and she found pleasures in camp life which she had not anticipated. Her husband was in a boat some distance out on the lake, and he was also fishing, but she did not care for that style of sport ; the fish were too big and the boat too small.

A little farther down the lake Martin Sanders sat busily engaged in putting some water-fowl into the foreground of Margery's sketch. A critical observer might have noticed that he had also made a number of changes in said sketch, all of which added greatly to its merits as a picture of woodland scenery. At a little distance Margery was sitting at her easel making a sketch of

Martin as an artist at work in the woods. The two young men had gone off with their guns, not perhaps because they expected to find any legitimate game at that season, but hoping to secure some ornithological specimens, or to get a shot at some minor quadrupeds unprotected by law. Another reason for their expedition could probably have been found in some strong hints given by Mr. Archibald that it was unwise for them to be hanging around the camps and taking no advantage of the opportunities for sport offered by the beautiful weather and the forest.

It was not long before Margery became convinced that the sketch on which she was working did not resemble her model, nor did it very much resemble an artist at work in the woods.

" It looks a good deal more like a cobbler mending shoes," she said to herself, "and I'll keep it for that. Some day I will put a bench under him and a shoe in his hand instead of a sketch." With that she rose, and went to see how Martin was getting on. " I think," she said, "those dark ducks improve the picture very much. They throw the other things back." Then she stopped, went to one side, and gazed out over the lake. "I wonder," she said, "if there is really any fun in fishing. Uncle Archibald has been out in that boat for more than two hours, and he has fished almost every day since he's been here. I should think he would get tired of it."

"Oh no," said Martin, looking up with animation. " If you know how to fish, and there is good sport, you never get tired of it."

53

"I know how to fish," said Margery, "and I do not care about it at all."

"You know how to fish?" said Martin. "Can you make a cast with a fly?"

"I never tried that," said she. "But I have fished as Aunt Harriet does, and it is easy as can be."

"Oh," said he, "you don't know anything about fishing unless you have fished with a fly. That is the only real sport. It is as exciting as a battle. If you would let me teach you how to throw a fly, I am sure you would never find fishing tiresome, and these woods would be like a new world to you."

"Why don't you do it yourself, then?" she asked.

"Because I am paid to do other things," he replied. "We are not sent here simply to enjoy ourselves, though I must say that I—" And then he suddenly stopped. "I wish you would let me teach you fly-fishing. I know you would like it."

Margery looked at the eager face turned towards her, and then she gazed out over the water.

"Perhaps I might like it," she said. "But it wouldn't be necessary for you to take that trouble. Uncle Archibald has two or three times asked me to go out with him, and of course he would teach me how to fish as he does. Isn't that somebody calling you?"

"Yes," said Martin, rising; "it's Phil. I suppose it's nearly supper-time."

As they walked towards the camp, Margery in front, and Martin behind her carrying the draw-

"'THEY THROW THE OTHER THINGS BACK'"

A. B. Frost.

ing - materials and the easel, Margery suddenly
turned.

" It was very good of you to offer to teach me
to fish with flies," she said, " and perhaps, if Uncle
Archibald doesn't want to be bothered, I may get
you to show me how to do it."

The young man's face brightened, and he was
about to express his pleasure with considerable
warmth ; but he checked himself, and merely remarked that whenever she was ready he would
provide a rod and flies and show her how to use
them.

Mrs. Archibald had gone into the cabin, and
Margery went up to Matlack, who was on his
way to the little•tent in which the camp cooking
was done.

" Did Mrs. Archibald tell you," said she, " that
we have invited Mr. Clyde and Mr. Raybold to
supper to-night ?"

The guide stopped and smiled. " She told me,"
said he, " but I don't know that it was altogether
necessary."

" I suppose you mean," said Margery, " that
they are here so much ; but I don't wonder ;
they must do awfully poor cooking for themselves. I don't suppose they will bring anything
back that is good to eat."

" Not at this time of year," said he, " but I
shall be satisfied if they bring themselves home."

" What do you mean by that ?" asked Margery,
quickly.

" Well," said Matlack, " I don't doubt the bicycle fellow will always come back all right, but
I'm afeard about the other one. That bicycle

chap don't know no more about a gun than he does about makin' bread, and I wouldn't go out huntin' with him for a hundred dollars. He's just as likely to take a crack at his pardner's head as at anything else that's movin' in the woods."

"That is dreadful!" exclaimed Margery.

"Yes, it is," returned the guide; "and if I had charge of their camp he wouldn't go out with a gun again. But it will be all right in a day or two. Peter will settle that."

"Mr. Sadler, do you mean?" asked Margery. "What's he got to do with it?"

"He's got everything to do with it," said Matlack. "He's got everything to do with everything in this part of the country. He's got his laws, and he sees to it that people stand by them. One of his rules is that people who don't know how to use guns sha'n't shoot in his camps."

"But how can he know about the people out here in the woods?" asked Margery.

"I tell you, miss," said Matlack, speaking slowly and decisively, "Peter Sadler's ways of knowing things is like gas—the kind you burn, I mean. I was a-visitin' once in a city house, and slept in a room on the top floor, and there was a leak in the pipe in the cellar, and that gas just went over the whole house, into every room and closet, and even under the beds, and I've often thought that that was just like Peter's way of doin' things and knowin' things. You take my word for it, that bicycle-man won't go out huntin' many more days, even if he don't shoot his pardner fust."

"He won't go to-morrow," thought Margery;

and then she said to Matlack : "I think we ought
to know Mr. Sadler's rules. Has he any more of
them ?"

"Oh, they ain't very many," said Matlack. "But
there's one I think of now, and that is that no woman shall go out in a boat by herself on this lake."

" That is simply horrid !" exclaimed Margery.
"Women can row as well as men."

" I don't say they can't," said Matlack. " I'm
only tellin' you what Peter's rules are, and that's
one of them."

Margery made no reply, but walked away, her
head thrown back a little more than was usual
with her.

" I've got to keep my eye on her," said Matlack
to himself, as he went to the cabin ; "she's never
been broke to no harness."

Mr. Raybold did not shoot Mr. Clyde, nor did
he shoot anything else. Mr. Clyde did shoot a
bird, but it fell into the water at a place where
the shore was very marshy, and it was impossible
for him to get it. He thought it was a heron,
or a bittern, or perhaps a fish-hawk, but whatever it was, both ladies said that it was a great
pity to kill it, as it was not good to eat, and must
have been very happy in its life in the beautiful
forest.

" It is very cruel to shoot them when they are
not strictly game," said Mr. Clyde, "and I don't
believe I will do it. If I had the things to stuff
them with, that would be different, but I haven't.
I believe fishing is just as much fun, and more
sensible."

"I do not!" exclaimed Mr. Raybold. "I hold that hunting is a manly art, and that a forester's life is as bold and free to him as it is to the birds in the air. I believe I have the blood of a hunter in me. My voice is for the woods."

"I expect you will change your voice," thought Margery, "when Mr. Sadler takes your gun away from you." But she did not say so.

Mr. Archibald stood with his hands in his pockets reflecting. He had hoped that these two young men were inveterate hunters, and that they would spend their days in long tramps. He did not at all approve of their fishing. Fishing could be done anywhere — here, for instance, right at this very door.

Supper was over, and the five inhabitants of Camps Rob and Roy had seated themselves around the fire which Martin had carefully built, keeping in view a cheery blaze without too much heat. Pipes had been filled and preparations made for the usual evening smoke and talk, when a man was seen emerging from the woods at the point where the road opened into the clearing about the camp. It was still light, for these hungry campers supped early, and the man could be distinctly seen as he approached, and it was plain that he was not a messenger from Sadler's.

He was rather a large man, dressed in black, and wearing a felt hat with a wide, straight brim. Hanging by a strap from his shoulder was a small leather bag, and in his hand he carried a closed umbrella. Advancing towards the fire, he took off his hat, bowed, and smiled. He wore no beard, his face was round and plump, and his smile was pleasant.

"Good-evening, ladies and gentlemen," said he, and his voice was as pleasant as his smile.

"Good-evening," said Mr. Archibald, and then for a moment there was a pause.

"I presume," said the new-comer, looking about him, "that this is a camp."

"It is a camp," said Mr. Archibald.

"The fact is so obvious," said the man in black, "that it was really unnecessary for me to allude to it. May I ask to be allowed to sit down for a few moments? I am fatigued."

At this juncture Phil Matlack arrived on the scene. "Well, sir," said he, "have you any business with anybody here? Who do you wish to see?"

"I have no business," said the other, "and—"

"And you are a stranger to everybody here?" interrupted Matlack.

"Yes, but I hope—"

"Now then," said the guide, quickly, "I've got to ask you to move on. This is one of Peter Sadler's camps, and he has strict rules against strangers stoppin' in any of them. If you've lost your way, I'll tell you that this road, if you don't turn to the right or the left, will take you straight to Sadler's, and there's time enough for you to get there before dark."

"Mr. Matlack," exclaimed Mrs. Archibald, who had risen to her feet, "I want to speak to you! It's a shame," she said, when the guide had approached her, "to send that man away without even giving him a chance to rest himself. He may be a very respectable person on a walking tour."

"I guess he is on a walkin' tour," said Matlack, "and I guess he's a regular tramp, and there's no orders we've got that's stricter than them against tramps."

"Well, I don't care who he is," said Mrs. Archibald, "or what your rules are, but when a perfectly good-mannered man comes to us and asks simply to be allowed to rest, I don't want him to be driven away as if he were a stray pig on a lawn. Mr. Archibald, shouldn't he be allowed to rest a while?"

Her husband rose and approached the stranger. "Where are you going, sir?" said he.

The man looked at Matlack, at Martin, who stood behind him, and then at the rest of the company, and after this comprehensive glance he smiled.

"From present appearances," he said, "I think I am going to go."

Mr. Archibald laughed. "When do you expect to get there?" he asked.

"It seems to me," said the other, reflectively, "that I am always going there, and I suppose I shall have to keep on doing it."

"Look here," said Mr. Archibald, turning to Matlack, "give him some supper, and let him rest. There will be time enough for him to get to Sadler's after that. If Sadler has anything to say against it, refer him to me."

"All right, sir," said Matlack, "if you say so. I'm no harder on my fellow-bein's than other people, but rules is rules, and it isn't for me to break them."

"My dear sir," said the stranger to Mr. Archibald, "your words are more grateful to me than the promise of food. I see that you consider me a tramp, but it is a mistake. I am not a tramp. If you will allow me, after I have eaten a little supper — a meal which I must admit I greatly need—I will explain to you how I happen to be here." And with a bow he walked towards the table where Matlack and Martin had been eating their supper.

"Do you know what I think he is?" said Mr. Clyde, when Mr. Archibald had resumed his seat and his pipe. "I believe he is a wandering actor. Actors always have smoothly shaven faces, and he looks like one."

"Actor!" exclaimed Arthur Raybold. "That's nonsense. He's not in the least like an actor. Anybody could see by his tread and his air that he's never been on the stage. He's more like a travelling salesman. The next thing he'll do will be to pull out of that bag some samples of spool thread or patent thimbles."

"You are both wrong," said Margery—"entirely wrong. I have been looking at him, and I believe he is a Methodist minister with a dead horse. They ride circuits, and of course when their horses die they walk. Just wait a little, and see if I am not right."

They waited a little, and then they waited a little longer, and they had begun to be tired of waiting before the stranger finished his meal and approached the fire. His face was brighter, his smile was more pleasant, and his step had a certain jauntiness in it.

"I thank you all," he said, "for the very good meal I have just enjoyed. I am now going to go, but before I start I would like very much—indeed, I crave it as a favor—to place myself before you in my proper light. May I have permission to do so, madam and sir?" he said, addressing Mrs. and Mr. Archibald, but with a respectful glance at the others, as if he would not ignore any one of them.

"Certainly," said Mrs. Archibald. "Sit down and tell us about yourself."

The stranger seated himself with alacrity a little back from the circle, and nearer to the young men than to the Archibald party.

THE stranger placed his broad-brimmed hat on the ground beside him, exposing a large round head somewhat bald in front, but not from age, and the rest of it covered with close-cut brown hair. His black clothes fitted him very closely, their extreme tightness suggesting that they had shrunken in the course of wearing, or that he had grown much plumper since he had come into possession of them ; and their general worn and dull appearance gave considerable distance to the period of their first possession. But there was nothing worn or dull about the countenance of the man, upon which was an expression of mellow geniality which would have been suitably consequent upon a good dinner with plenty of wine. But his only beverage had been coffee, and in his clear bright eye there was no trace of any exhilaration, except that caused by the action of a hearty meal upon a good digestion and an optimistic disposition.

"I am very glad," he said, looking about him at the company, and then glancing with a friendly air towards the two guides, who stood a little back of Mr. Archibald, "to have this opportunity to explain my appearance here. In the first place,

I must tell you that I am a bishop whose diocese has been inundated, and who consequently has been obliged to leave it."

"Oh!" exclaimed Mr. Archibald; and Margery looked at Mr. Clyde, with the remark:

"There! You see I was very near to it."

"I presume this statement will require some explanation," continued the man in black, "and I will make it presently. I am going to be exceedingly frank and open in all that I say to you, and as frankness and openness are so extremely rare in this world, it may be that I shall obtain favor in your eyes from the fact of my possessing those unusual qualities. Originally I was a teacher, and for a year or two I had a very good country school; but my employment at last became so repugnant to me that I could no longer endure it, and this repugnance was due entirely to my intense dislike for children."

"That is not at all to your credit," observed Mrs. Archibald; "and I do not see how you became a bishop, or why you should have been made one."

"Was your diocese entirely meadow-land?" inquired Mr. Archibald.

"I am coming to all that," said the stranger, with a smile of polite consideration towards Mrs. Archibald. "I know very well that it is not at all to my credit to dislike children, but I said I would be honest, and I am. I do dislike them— not their bodies, but their minds. Children, considered physically, are often pleasant to the view, and even interesting as companions, providing their innate juvenility is undisturbed; but when

64

their personalities are rudely thrown open by a teacher, and the innate juvenility prematurely exposed to the air, it is something so clammy, so chilly to the mental marrow, that I shrink from it as I would shrink from the touch of any cold, clammy thing."

"Horrible!" exclaimed Mrs. Archibald.

"I am not sure," observed Margery, "that there is not some truth in that. I had a Sunday-school class for a little while, and although I can't say there was a clamminess, there was—well, I don't know what there was, but I gave it up."

"I am glad," said the man in black, "that my candor is not sinking me in the estimation of every one present; but even if it did, I am obliged to tell the truth. I do not know what would have become of me if I had not had the good-fortune to catch the measles from a family with whom I was spending Sunday in another town. As soon as the disease plainly showed itself upon me my school was broken up, and it was never gathered together again, at least under me.

"I must make my story brief, and can only say that not long after this I found myself in another town, where it became necessary for me to do something to support myself. This was difficult, for I am an indefinite man, and definiteness seems necessary to success in any line. Happening one day to pass a house with open lower windows, I heard the sound of children's voices speaking in unison, and knowing that this must be a school, I looked in, compelled entirely by that curiosity which often urges us to gaze upon human suffering. I found, however, that this was a kindergarten conducted by a young woman. Unobserved by scholars or teacher, I watched the proceedings with great interest, and soon became convinced that kindergartening was a much less repellent system of tuition than any I had known; but I also perceived that the methods of the young woman could be greatly improved. I thought a good deal upon this subject after leaving the open window. Soon afterwards, becoming acquainted with the young person in charge of the children, I offered to teach her a much better system of kindergartening than she was using. My terms were very low, and she became my scholar. I soon learned that there were other kindergartens in the town, and some of the teachers of these joined my class. Moreover, there were young women in the place who were not kindergartners, but who would like to become such, and these I also taught, sometimes visiting them at their houses, and sometimes giving my lessons in a room loaned by one of my patrons. My system became very popular, because it was founded upon common-sense."

"What was your system?" asked Mrs. Archibald. "I am interested in kindergartens myself."

" My object," he answered, "was to make the operation of teaching interesting to the teacher. It struck me very forcibly that a continuance of a few years in the present inane performances called kindergartening would infallibly send to our lunatic asylums a number of women, more or less young, with more or less depleted intellects. The various games and exercises I devised were very interesting, and I am sure I had scholars who never intended to become kindergartners, and who studied with me solely for their own advantage. It was at this time that I adopted the clerical dress as being more suitable to my vocation than any other costume, and some one having called me the bishop, the name soon became popular, and I was generally known by it."

" But what is your real name ?" asked Mrs. Archibald.

"Madam," said the man, "you must excuse me if I ask you to recall your question. I have a good name, and I belong to a very good family, but there are reasons why I do not at present wish to avow that name. Some of these reasons are connected with the report that I purposely visited the family with the measles in order to get rid of my school; others are connected with the inundation of my diocese, of which I shall speak ; others refer to my present indefinite method of life. There is reason to suppose that the time is not far distant when my resumption of my family name will throw no discredit upon it, but that period has not yet arrived. Do you press your question, madam ?"

" Oh no," said Mrs. Archibald; "it really makes no difference ; and out here in the woods a man may call himself a bishop or a cardinal or anything he likes."

" Thank you very much," said he, "and I will continue to speak in figures, and call myself a bishop."

" Where I was brought up," interpolated Phil Matlack, still standing behind Mr. Archibald, " I was taught that figures don't lie."

"My good sir," said the speaker, with a smile, "in mathematics they don't, in poetry and literature they often do. Well, as I was saying, my diocese extended itself, my revenues were satisfactory, and I had begun to believe that I had found my true work in life, when suddenly there was a misfortune. There arrived in our town three apostles of kindergartening—two of them were women, and one was a man. They had heard of my system, and had come to investigate it. They did so, with the result that in an astonishingly short time my diocese was inundated with a flood of Froebelism which absolutely swept me away. With this bag, this umbrella, and this costume, which has now become my wardrobe, I was cast out in all my indefiniteness upon a definite world."

"And how did you get here?" asked Mrs. Archibald.

"I had heard of Sadler and his camps," said he; "and in this beautiful month and in this beautiful weather I thought it would be well to investigate them. I accordingly went to Mr. Sadler's, where I arrived yesterday afternoon. I found Mr. Sadler a very definite man, and, I am sorry to say, that as he immediately defined me as a tramp, he would listen to no other definition. 'You have no money to pay for food and lodgings,' said he, 'and you come under my tramp laws. I don't harbor tramps, but I don't kick them out into the woods to starve. For labor on this place I pay one dollar and a half a day of ten hours. For meals to day-laborers I charge fifteen cents each. If you want your supper, you can go out to that wood-shed and split wood for one hour.' I was very hungry; I went out into the wood-shed ; I split wood for one hour, and at the end of that time I had a sufficient meal. When I had finished, Mr. Sadler sent for me. 'Do you want to stay here all night ?' he said. ' I do,' I answered. 'Go, then, and split wood for another hour.' I did so, and it was almost dark when I had finished. In the morning I split wood for my breakfast, and when I had finished I went to Mr. Sadler and asked him how much he would charge for a luncheon wrapped in a piece of paper. 'Seven and a half cents,' he said. I split wood for half an hour, and left Sadler's ostensibly to return to the station by the way I had come; but while I had been at work, I found from the conversation of some of the people that one of the camps was occupied, and I also discovered in what direction it lay. Consequently, after I had passed out of the sight of the definite Peter Sadler, I changed my course, and took a path through the woods which I was told would lead to this road, and I came here because I might just as well pass this way as any other, and because, having set out to investigate camp life, I wished to do so, and I hope I may be allowed to say that although I have seen but little of it, I like it very much."

"Now, then," said Phil Matlack, walking around the circle and approaching the stranger, "you said, when you first came here, that you were going to go, and the time has come when you've got to go."

"Very well," said the other, looking up with a smile ; "if I've got there I'd better stop."

Mr. Archibald and the young men laughed, but Matlack and Martin, who had now joined him, did not laugh.

"You've barely time enough," said the former, "to get to Sadler's before it is pitch-dark, and—"

"Excuse me," said the other, "but I am not going back to Sadler's to-night. I would rather have no bed than split wood for an hour after dark in order to procure one. I would prefer a couch of dried leaves."

"You come along into the road with this young man and me; I want to talk to you," said Matlack.

"Now, Matlack," said Mr. Archibald, "don't be cruel."

"I am not," said the guide. "I am the tenderest-hearted person in the world; but even if you say so, sir, I can't let a stranger stay all night in a camp that I've got charge of."

"Look here, Matlack," exclaimed Mr. Clyde, "you haven't got charge of our camp!"

"No, I haven't," said the other.

"Well, then, this person can come over and stay with us. We have a little tent that we brought to put over the cooking-stove, and he can sleep in that."

"Very well," said Matlack; "if you take him out of this camp I haven't anything to say—that is, to-night."

"My dear sir," said the stranger, rising, and approaching Mr. Clyde, "I accept your offer with pleasure, and thank you most heartily for it. If you had proffered me the hospitality of a palace, I could not be more grateful."

"All right," said Clyde; "and I suppose it is time for us to be off, so I will bid you all good-night. Come along, Arthur. Come along, bishop."

The face of the last-named individual beamed with delight as he heard this appellation, and bidding everybody good-night, and thanking them for the kindness with which he had been treated, he followed the two young men.

The three walked some little distance towards Camp Roy, and then Clyde came running back to speak to Margery, who was now standing by herself watching the young moon descend among the trees. Then Mr. Raybold also stopped and came back to Margery, upon which the bishop stopped and waited for them. In about ten minutes he was joined by the two young men, and the three proceeded to Camp Roy.

"There is one thing, Harriet," said Mr. Archibald, "which I wish you would speak to Margery about. I don't want her to get up so early and go out for a morning walk. I find that those young men are also early risers."

"I will speak to her," said Mrs. Archibald; "where is she?"

"Over there, talking to young Martin," said her husband. "It isn't quite dark yet, but I think it is time we were all in bed."

"Quite time," said she. "Margery tells me that that young guide, who is a handsome fellow, is going to teach her how to fish with flies. I wish you would sometimes take her out in the boat with you, Mr. Archibald; I am sure that you could teach her how to fish."

He smiled. "I suppose I could," he said; "and

I also suppose I could pull her out of the water the first time she hooked a big fish. It would be like resting a boat on a pivot to put her into it."

" Then you don't take her," said Mrs. Archibald, decisively. "And you can't take her with you up the stream, because, of course, she can't wade. I don't want her to get tired of camp-life, but—"

" Don't be afraid of the young men," interrupted her husband, with a laugh ; "so long as there are three of them there is no danger."

"Of course I will not, if you don't wish it, Aunt Harriet," said Margery, when Mrs. Archibald had spoken to her about the early morning walks ; "and I will stay in my room until you call me."

The next morning, when Mrs. Archibald was ready to leave the cabin, she did call Margery, but received no answer. Then she went to the little studio-room, and when she opened the door she found its occupant leaning out of the window talking to Mr. Clyde and Mr. Raybold, who stood outside.

" Good - morning, Aunt Harriet !" exclaimed Margery, gayly. "Mr. Clyde has brought me nearly an armful of birch - bark, all thin and smooth. I am going to make a birch-bark bedspread out of it. I'll cover a sheet with these pieces, you see, and sew them on. Then I can have autographs on them, and mottoes, and when I cover myself up with it I shall really feel like a dryad."

" And here is what I have brought," said Mr. Raybold, holding up an armful of bark.

"Oh, thank you very much," said Margery, taking the mass, but not without dropping a good many of the pieces. "Of course it was kind of him to bring it," she said to Mrs. Archibald, as they left the room together, " but he needn't have bothered himself : I don't want to sleep under a wood-pile."

CHAPTER IX

MATLACK'S THREE TROUBLES

"Have you asked those two young men to breakfast again?" inquired Mr. Archibald, after examining, with a moderate interest, the specimen of birch-bark which Margery had shown him.

"Oh no, indeed," said she, "they have had their breakfast. They have been telling me about it. The bishop got up very early in the morning and cooked it for them. He's a splendid cook, and he found things in their hampers that they didn't know they had. They said his coffee was delicious, and they have left him there in their camp now, washing the dishes and putting everything in order. And do you think, Uncle Archibald, that it is going to rain?"

"I do," said he, "for it is sprinkling already."

This proved to be the first bad day since the Archibald party had gone into camp, and the rain soon began to come down in a steady, practised way, as if the clouds above were used to that sort of thing and could easily keep it up all day.

As there was no place under roof to which company could be conveniently invited, Margery retired to her room and set herself diligently to work on her birch-bark quilt.

Mrs. Archibald established herself in the division of the cabin which was intended to be used as a sitting and dining room in bad weather, and applied herself to some sewing and darning, which had been reserved for just such a day as this. Mr. Archibald, in a water-proof suit, tried fishing for half an hour or so, but finding it both unpleasant and unprofitable, he joined his wife, made himself as comfortable as possible on two chairs, and began to read aloud one of the novels they had brought with them.

Mr. Clyde and Mr. Raybold had considerately gone to their own camp when it began to rain, hoping, however, that the shower would be over in a short time. But the rain was not a shower, and they spent the morning on their backs in their tent, talking and smoking. Of course they could not expect the bishop to depart in the rain, so they had told him to make himself as comfortable as he could in the little kitchen tent, and offered him a pipe and a book. The first he declined, as he never smoked, but the latter he accepted with delight.

After the mid-day dinner Phil Matlack, in a pair of high hunting-boots and an oil-skin coat, came to Mr. Archibald and said that as there was nothing he could do that afternoon, he would walk over to Sadler's and attend to some business he had there.

" About the bishop?" asked Mr. Archibald.

" Partly," said Matlack. " I understand the fellow is still over there with those two young men. I don't suppose they'll send him off in the rain, and as he isn't in my camp, I can't interfere. But it may rain for two or three days."

"All right," said Mr. Archibald, "and if we want anything we'll ask Martin."

"Just so," said Matlack. "If there's anything to do that you don't want to do yourself, you can get him to do it; but if you want to know anything you don't know yourself, you'd better wait until I come back."

When Matlack presented himself before Peter Sadler he found that ponderous individual seated in his rolling-chair near the open door, enjoying the smell of the rain.

"Hello, Phil!" he cried. "What's wrong at the camp?"

The guide left his wet coat and cap on the little piazza outside, and after carefully wiping his feet, seated himself on a chair near the door.

"There's three things wrong," said he. "In the first place, there's a tramp out there, and it looks to me as if he was a-goin' to stick, if he can get allowed to do it."

"Is he too big for you to bounce?" roared Peter. "That's a pretty story to come tell me!"

"No, he ain't," said the other; "but I haven't got the bouncin' of him. He's not in my camp. The young men have took him in; but I expect he'll come over with them as soon as it's done rainin', for when that happens they're bound to come themselves."

"Look here, Phil," said Peter, "is he dressed in black?"

"Yes, he is," said the guide.

Mr. Sadler slapped his hand on the arm of his chair. "Phil Matlack," he shouted, "that's my favorite tramp. I never had a man here who

paid his bill in work as he did. It was cash down,
and good money. Not a minute of wood-split-
ting more or less than the market-price for meals
and bed. I'd like to have a tramp like that come
along about twice a week. But I tell you, Phil,
he ain't no tramp. Couldn't you see that? None
of them loafers ever worked as he did."

"He may not be a tramp," said Matlack, "but
he's trampin'. What are you goin' to do about
him? Let him stay there?"

"What's he doin' now?" asked Sadler.

, "He's cookin' for those two young men."

"Well, they need some one to do it for them,
and they didn't want to go to the expense of a
guide. Let the parson alone for a day or two,
and if he does anything out of the way just you
take him by one ear and Martin take him by the
other and bring him to me. I'll attend to him.
What's the next trouble?"

"That's out of my camp, too," said Matlack,
"but I'm bound to report it. The bicycle fellow
that you hired a gun to don't know the fust thing
about usin' it, and the next thing you'll hear will
be that he's shot his pardner, who's worth six of
him."

Mr. Sadler sat up very straight in his chair
and stared at the guide. "Phil Matlack," he
shouted, "what do you take me for? I hired that
gun to that young man. Don't you suppose I
know what I'm about?"

"That's all right," said Matlack, "but the
trouble is he don't know what he's about."

"Get away man," said Peter, with a contempt-
uous sniff, "he'll never hurt anybody. What

77

do you take me for? When he came to me and wanted a gun, I handed him two or three, so that he might choose one that suited him, and by the way he handled them I could see that most likely he'd never handled one before, and so I set him up all right. He's got a good gun, and all the cartridges he'll be likely to want; and the cartridges are all like this. They're a new kind I heard of last winter, and I got a case from Boston last week. I don't see how I ever managed to run my camps without them. Do you see that shot?" said he, opening one end of a cartridge. "Well, take one in your hand and pinch it."

Phil did so, and it crumbled to dust in his hand.

"When that load's fired," said Peter, "all the shot will crumble into dust. It wouldn't do to give raw hands blank-cartridges, because they'd find that out; but with this kind they might sit all day and fire at a baby asleep in its cradle and never disturb it, provided the baby was deaf. And he can't use his pardner's cartridges, for I gave that fellow a twelve-bore gun and his is a ten-bore."

Phil grinned. "Well, then," said he, "I suppose I might as well make my mind easy, but if that bicycle man hunts much he'll get the conviction borne in on him that he's a dreadful bad shot."

"Then he'll give up shooting, which is what is wanted," said Sadler. "What's your third bother?"

"That young woman has made up her mind to go out in the boat by herself the very fust time

she feels like it," said Matlack; "she didn't say so
with her mouth, but she said it with the back of
her head and her shoulders, and I want to know
if that rule of yours is going to hold good this
summer. Women is gettin' to do so many things
they didn't use to that I didn't know but what
you'd consider they'd got far enough to take
themselves out on the lake, and if you do think
so, I don't want to get myself in hot water with
those people and then find you don't back me up."

"If you don't want to get yourself into hot
water with me, Phil Matlack, you'd better get it
into your head just as soon as you can that when
I make a rule it's a rule, and I don't want people
comin' to me and talkin' about changes. Women
in my camp don't go out in boats by themselves,
and it's easy enough to have that rule kept if
you've got backbone enough to do it. Keep the
boat locked to the shore when it ain't in use, and
put the key in your pocket, and if anybody gets
it that 'ain't any right to it, that's your lookout.
Now that's the end of your troubles, I hope.
How's things goin' on generally in the camp?"

"Oh, well enough," said Matlack. "I thought
at fust the old lady'd give out in a day or two,
but I've taught her parlor-fishin', which she's
took to quite lively, and she's got used to the
woods. The boss, he sticks to fishin', as if it was
office-work, and as for the rest of them, I guess
they're all gettin' more and more willin' to stay."

"Why?" asked Peter.

"Well, one of them is a gal and the others isn't,"
replied Matlack, "that's about the p'int of it."

During Matlack's walk back the skies cleared,

and when he reached the camp he found Mrs. Archibald seated in her chair near the edge of the lake, a dry board under her feet, and the bishop standing by her, putting bait on her hook, and taking the fish off of it when any happened to be there. Out in the boat sat Mr. Archibald, trusting that some fish might approach the surface in search of insects disabled by the rain. Farther on, at a place by the water's edge that was clear of bushes and undergrowth, Martin was giving Miss Dearborn a lesson in fly-fishing.

"He's a mighty good fisherman," thought Matlack, looking at the young fellow as he brought his rod back from the water with a long graceful sweep, and then, with another sweep and an easy inclination of his body forward, sending the fly far out on the smooth surface of the lake, "although there ain't no need to tell him so; and I don't wonder she'd rather stand and watch him than try to do it herself."

Walking up and down near the edge of the wood were Messrs. Clyde and Raybold.

Phil smiled. "They don't seem to be happy," he said to himself. "I guess they're hankerin' to take a share in her edication; but if you don't know nothin' yourself, you can't edicate other people."

Matlack directed his steps towards Mrs. Archibald; but before he reached her he was met by the bishop, who hurried towards him.

"I shall be obliged to surrender my post to you," he said, "which will be greatly to the lady's satisfaction, I imagine, for I must appear a poor attendant after you."

"A LESSON IN FLY - FISHING"

"Goin' to leave us?" said Matlack. "You look quite spruced up."

The bishop smiled. "You allude, I suppose," said he, "to the fact that my hat and clothes are brushed, and that I am freshly shaved and have on a clean collar. I like to be as neat as I can. This is a gutta-percha collar, and I can wash it whenever I please with a bit of damp rag, and it is my custom to shave every day, if I possibly can. But as to leaving you, I shall not do so this evening. I have promised those young gentlemen who so kindly invited me to their camp that I would prepare their supper for them, and I must now go to make the fire and get things in readiness."

"Have they engaged you as cook and general help?" asked Matlack.

"Oh no," said the bishop, with a smile, "they are kind and I am grateful, that is all."

CHAPTER X

A LADIES' DAY IN CAMP

Two days after the rainy day in camp Mr. Archibald determined to take the direction of affairs into his own hands, so far as he should be able. Having no authority over the two young men at Camp Roy, he had hitherto contented himself with a disapproval of their methods of employing their time, which he communicated only to his wife. But now he considered that, as they were spending so much of their time in his camp and so little in their own, he would take charge of them exactly as if they belonged to his party. He would put an end, if possible, to the aimless strolls up and down the beach with Margery, and the long conversations of which that young woman had grown to be so fond, held sometimes with both young men, though more frequently with one. If Clyde and Raybold came into the woods to lounge in the shade and talk to a girl, they must go to some other camp to do it. But if they really cared to range the forest, either as sportsmen or lovers of nature, he would do his best to help them; so this day he organized an expedition to a low mountain about two miles away, taking Matlack with him as guide, and inviting the two young men to join him. They

82

had assented because no good reason for declin-
ing had presented itself, and because Phil Matlack earnestly urged them to come along and let
him show them what a real forest tramp was
like. Before his recent talk with Peter Sadler,
Phil would not have dared to go out into the
woods in company with the bicycle man.

The two ladies were perfectly willing to remain
in camp under the charge of Martin, who was
capable of defending them against any possible
danger; and as the bishop had agreed to take
charge of Camp Roy during the absence of its
occupants, Mr. Archibald planned for a whole
day's tramp, the first he had taken since they
went into camp.

When Martin's morning work was done he approached the shady spot where the two ladies had
established themselves, and offered to continue
his lessons in fish-flying if Miss Dearborn so desired. But Miss Dearborn did not wish to take
any lessons to-day. She would rest and stay
with Mrs. Archibald. Even the elder lady did
not care to fish that morning. The day was hot
and the shade was grateful.

Martin walked away dissatisfied. In his opinion, there had never been a day more suitable
for angling; this was a day which would be free
from interruptions, either from two young fellows who knew nothing about real game-fishing,
or from Matlack, who always called him away to
do something when he was most interested in his
piscatorial pedagogics. This was a day when he
could stand by that lovely girl, give her the rod,
show her how to raise it, wave it, and throw it,

and sometimes even touch her hand as he took it from her or gave it back, watching her all the time with an admiration and delight which no speckled trout or gamy black bass had ever yet aroused in him, and all this without fear that a gentleman out on the lake might possibly be observing them with the idea that he was more interested in his work than the ordinary guide might be supposed to be. But luck was against him, and Martin, who did not in the least consider himself an ordinary guide, walked up and down in moody reflection, or grimly threw himself upon the ground, gazing upward at the sky—not half so blue as he was—but never walking or resting so far away that he could not hear the first cry from her should snake, bear, dragon-fly, or danger of any kind approach her.

To the ladies, about half an hour later, came the bishop, who, newly shaved and brushed, wished them good-morning, and offered his services in any manner which might be desired. If Mrs. Archibald wished to fish by the side of the lake, he was at her service; but Mrs. Archibald did not care to fish.

"This is a most charming day," said the bishop, removing his hat, "but I suppose it is more charming to me because it is my last day here."

"And so you are really going to go?" said Mrs. Archibald, smiling.

"I suppose you think I am not likely to get there," said he, "but really I have stayed here long enough, and for several reasons."

"Sit down," said Margery, "and tell us what
84

they are. There is a nice little rock with some moss on it."

The bishop promptly accepted the invitation and seated himself. As he did so, Martin, at a little distance, scowled, folded his arms, and slightly increased the length of his sentinel-like walk.

"Yes," said the bishop, brushing some pine leaves from his threadbare trousers, "during the time that I have accepted the hospitality of those young gentlemen I feel that I have in a great measure repaid them for their kindness, but now I see that I shall become a burden and an expense to them. In the first place, I eat a great deal more than both of them put together, so that the provisions they brought with them will be exhausted much sooner than they expected. I am also of the opinion that they are getting tired of eating in their own camp, but as I make a point of preparing the meals at stated hours, of course they feel obliged to partake of them."

"By which you mean, I suppose," said Mrs. Archibald, "that if they had not you to cook for them they would be apt to take a good many meals with us, as they did when they first came, and which would be cheaper and pleasanter."

"I beg, madam," said the bishop, quickly, "that you will not think that they have said anything of the sort. I simply inferred, from remarks I have heard, that one of them, at least, is very much of the opinion you have just stated ; therefore I feel that I cannot be welcome much longer in Camp Roy. There is also another reason why I should go now. I have a business prospect before me."

"I am glad to hear that," said Mrs. Archibald. "Is it a good one?"

"I think it is," said the bishop. "I have been considering it earnestly, and the more I fix my mind upon it the greater appear its advantages. I don't mind in the least telling you what it is. A gentleman who is acquainted with my family and whom I have met two or three times, but not recently, possesses a very fine estate some thirty miles south of this place. He has been in Europe for some time, but is expected to return to his country mansion about the end of this week. It is my purpose to offer myself to him in the capacity of private librarian. I do not think it will be difficult to convince him that I have many qualifications for the situation."

"Has he so many books that he needs a librarian?" asked Margery.

"No," said the bishop, "I have no reason to suppose that he has any more books than the ordinary country gentleman possesses, but he ought to have. He has a very large income, and is now engaged in establishing for his family what is intended to become, in time, an ancestral mansion. It is obvious to any one of intelligence that such a grand mansion would not be complete without a well-selected library, and that such a library could not be selected or arranged by an ordinary man of affairs. Consequently, unless he has a competent person to perform this duty for him, his library, for a long time, will be insignificant. When I shall put the question before him, I have no doubt that he will see and appreciate the force and value of my statements. Such a position

will suit me admirably. I shall ask but little sal-
ary, but it will give me something far better than
money—an opportunity to select from the book
marts of the whole world the literature in which
I delight. Consequently, you will see that it is
highly desirable that I should be on hand when
this gentleman arrives upon his estate."

With a look of gentle pity Mrs. Archibald gazed
at the smooth round face of the bishop, flushed
with the delights of anticipation and brightened
by the cheery smile which nearly always accompanied his remarks. "And is that your only prospect?" she said. "I don't want to discourage
you, but it seems to me that if you had some regular business—and you are not too old to learn
something of the sort—it would be far better for
you than trying to obtain the mythical position
you speak of. I see that you are a man of intelligence and education, and I believe that you
would succeed in almost any calling to which you
would apply yourself with earnestness and in-
dustry. You must excuse me for speaking so
plainly, but I am much older than you are and I
do it for your good."

"Madam," exclaimed the bishop, radiant with
grateful emotion, "I thank you from the bottom
of my heart for what you have said. I thank you
for your appreciation of me and for the generous
motive of your words, but, to be frank with you,
I am not suited to a calling such as you have
mentioned. I have many qualities which I well
know would promote my fortunes were they
properly applied, but that application is difficult,
for the reason that my principal mental character-

istic is indefiniteness. When but a little child I was indefinite. Nobody knew what I was going to do, or how I would turn out; no one has since known, and no one knows now. In whatever way I have turned my attention in my endeavors to support myself, I have been obstructed and even appalled by the definiteness of the ordinary pursuits of life. Now the making of a private library is in itself an indefinite occupation. It has not its lines, its rules, its limitations. But do not think, kind lady, that I shall always depend upon such employment. Should I obtain it, I should hold it only so long as it would be necessary, and it may be necessary for but a little while. Do you care to hear of my permanent prospects?" said he, looking from one lady to the other.

"Certainly," said Margery, "we would like to hear all you have to tell."

"Well then," said the bishop, folding his arms and smiling effusively, but with a gentle curbing of his ordinary cheerfulness, "I will inform you that I have an uncle who is a man of wealth and well on in years. Unfortunately, or fortunately it may be, this uncle greatly dislikes me. He objects so strongly to my methods of thought and action, and even to my physical presence, that he cannot bear to hear me speak or even to look at me, and the last time I was in his company, about four years ago, he told me that he would leave me a legacy on condition that he should never hear from me or see me again. He promised to make the proper provision in his will immediately, but declared, and I know he will keep his word, that if he ever received a letter

88

from me or even saw me or heard my voice he would instantly strike out that clause. I appreciated and respected his feelings, and accepted the condition. From that moment I have not written to him, nor shall I ever write to him, and I shall never go near him so long as he is alive. As I said, he is of advanced age, and it is impossible that he can long survive. When his demise takes place my circumstances will, I believe, be satisfactory."

" Did your uncle say how much he would leave you ?" asked Mrs. Archibald.

" No, madam," returned the other, " he did not, but I feel sure that the sum will be measured by his satisfaction in knowing that his existence is entirely freed from me."

" Really," said Mrs. Archibald, " there is nothing about you so indefinite as your prospects."

" And it seems horrible to me," said Margery, " to be hoping that some one may die in order that you may be better off, for, as you want money so much, you must hope that your uncle will die."

The bishop smiled and rose. " And now," said he, " I suppose I must go to prepare the dinner at Camp Roy. There is nobody but myself to eat it, but I have assumed the duty, and it must be performed. Good-morning. By your leave, I shall look in upon you again."

Mrs. Archibald had a mind to ask him to stay and dine with them, but having noticed an unfriendly expression on the face of Martin when his gloomy walk brought him in her direction, she thought it would not be wise to do so.

89

CHAPTER XI

MARGERY TAKES THE OARS

AFTER dinner Mrs. Archibald prepared herself for a nap, the most delightful thing she could think of during the warm hours of such a day. Margery, after seeing the elder lady comfortably disposed in the shady sitting-room of the cabin, went out-of-doors with no doubt in her mind as to what would be for her the most delightful thing to do. She would take a row on the lake all by herself.

She went down to the boat, which was partly drawn up on the beach and fastened to a heavy stake. But when she reached it she was disgusted to find that the chain was secured to the stake by a padlock. The oars were in the boat, and she could easily have pushed it into the water, but she could not set it free without the key to the padlock.

"I do believe," she exclaimed, "that the will of that horrid Mr. Sadler is like gas. It goes everywhere, even to the tops of the houses and under the beds." But she did not give up her intention. She tried to detach the chain from the boat, but finding this impossible, she thought of going for Martin. Perhaps he might have a key. This idea, however, she quickly put aside. If he

had a key, and gave it to her, she might get him
into trouble, and, besides, she did not believe that
he would let her go alone, and in any other way
she did not wish to go. Standing with her pretty
brows knit, and one heel deep in the soft ground
into which she had stamped it, she heard approaching footsteps, and turning, saw the bishop.
He came forward with a buoyant step.

"Is there anything I can do for you, Miss Dearborn?" he said. "Do you wish to go out on the
lake? Do you want some one to row you?"

"Yes and no," said Margery. "I want to go
out in the boat, and I don't want anybody to row
me. But that chain is fastened with an abomi-
nable padlock, and I cannot launch the boat."

"One of your guides is here," said he. "Perhaps I can get a key from him."

"No, no," said Margery, quickly; "he must not
know about it. There is a Sadler law against it,
and he is employed by Sadler."

"It is very securely fastened," said the bishop,
examining the lock and chain. "It is the work
of the guide Matlack, I have no doubt. But,
Miss Dearborn," said he, with a bright smile,
"there is a boat at Camp Roy. That is not
locked, and I can bring it here in twenty minutes."

"No," said Margery; "I don't want that boat.
I've seen it. It is a clumsy old thing, and, besides, it leaks. I want this one. This is just the
kind of boat I want to row. It is too bad! If I
could get off now there would be nobody to hin-
der me, for Martin is washing the dinner dishes,
or doing something of that kind, and whenever

he does house-work he always keeps himself out of sight."

The bishop examined the stake. It was a stout little tree trunk driven deep into the ground and projecting about five feet above the surface, with the chain so wrapped around it that it was impossible to force it up or down. Seizing the stake near the top, the bishop began to push it backward and forward, and being a man of great strength, he soon loosened it so much that, stooping, he was able to pull it from the ground.

"Hurrah !" exclaimed Margery. "It came up just like pulling a tooth."

"Yes," said the radiant bishop, "the good Matlack may be very careful about fastening a boat, but I think I have got the better of him this time ; and now I will put the stake, chain and all, in the bow. That is the best way of disposing of them. Are you sure that you prefer going alone ? I shall be delighted to row you if you wish me to."

"Oh no," said Margery ; "I am just wild to row myself, and I want to hurry and get off for fear Martin will be coming down here."

"Are you sure you understand rowing and the management of a boat ?" he asked.

"Oh yes," she replied, "I can row ; of course I can. I will get in, and then you can push off the boat."

"Allow me," said the bishop. But before he could reach her to help her, Margery stepped quickly into the boat and was about to seat herself.

"If you will take the seat next to the stern,"

said the bishop, holding the boat so that it would
be steady, "I think that will be better. Then the
weight of the stake in the bow will put the boat
on an even keel."

"All right," said Margery, accepting his suggestion and seating herself. "Now just wait
until I get the oars into the rowlocks, and then
you can push me off."

"Which way do you intend to row?" asked the
bishop.

"Oh, I shall go down towards the lower end of
the lake, because that way there are more bushes
along the banks and Martin will be less apt to see
me. If I go the other way I will be in plain sight
of the camp, and he may think he ought to do
something—fire a gun across my bows to bring
me to, maybe, as they do at sea."

"Hardly," said the bishop, "but let me ad-
vise you not to go very far from the shore, so
that if you feel tired you can come in easily,
and if you will allow me I will walk down the
shore in the direction in which you intend to
row."

"Oh, I am not going to get tired," said she.
"I could row all day. It is splendid to be in a
boat all by myself and have the whole management of it. Now please push me off."

With some reluctance, but with a sincere desire
to make the young girl happy, which could not
be overcome by prudence—at least by such prudence as he possessed—the bishop, with a strong,
steady push, sent the boat well out on the surface
of the water.

"That was beautifully done," Margery called

back to him. "Now I have room enough to turn around without any trouble at all."

She turned the boat about with its bow towards the lower end of the lake, but it was not done without trouble. "I have not rowed for a good while," she said, "but I am getting used to the oars already. Now then, I'm off," and she began to pull with a strength which, had it been suitably paired with skill, would have made her an excellent amateur oarswoman. But the place of skill was supplied by enthusiasm and determination. Once or twice an oar slipped from the rowlock and she nearly went over backward, and several times one of the blades got under the water with the flat side up, so that she had difficulty in getting it out. She raised her oars much too high in the air, but she counterbalanced this by sinking them very deep into the water. But she got on, and although her course was somewhat irregular, its general trend was in the direction desired.

The bishop walked along the bank, keeping as near to the water as he could. Sometimes masses of shrubbery shut off all view of the lake, and then there would be an open space where he would stop and watch the boat.

"Please keep near the shore, Miss Dearborn," he called, "that will be better, I think, and it is certainly more shady and pleasant than farther out."

"I know what you mean," cried Margery, pulling away in high good-humor, "you think it is safer near the shore; but I am not going to row very far this time, and after a little while I may

pull the boat in and rest for a time before starting back," and then she rowed on with renewed
energy.

The next time the bishop was able to hail the
boat, it was at a point where he was obliged to
push his way through the bushes in order to see
out upon the lake.

" Miss Dearborn," he called, "I think you are a
great deal too far from shore, and you must be
getting very tired and hot. Your face is greatly
flushed. I will hurry along and see if I can find
a good place for you to stop and cool yourself."

"I am all right," cried Margery, resting on her
oars. "I get along very well, only the boat
doesn't steer properly. I think it is because of
the weight of that stick in the bow. I suppose I
cannot get rid of it ?"

"Oh no !" cried the bishop, in alarm ; "please
don't think of it ! But if you touch shore at the
first open space, I think I can arrange it better
for you."

"Very good," said she ; "you go ahead and find
such a place, and I will come in."

"If you touch shore," said the bishop to himself, "you don't go out again in that boat alone !
You don't know how to row at all."

The bishop ran a hundred yards or more before
he found a place at which a boat could be beached.
It was not a very good place, but if he could reach
out and seize the bow, that would be enough
for him. He was strong enough to pull that boat
over a paved street.

As he looked out over the water he saw that
Margery had progressed considerably since he

had seen her last, but she was still farther from shore than before.

"Row straight towards me!" he shouted. "Here is a fine landing-place, cool and shady."

She looked around and managed to turn the boat's head in his direction. Then she rowed hard, pulling and splashing, and evidently a little tired. She was strong, but this unusual exercise was a trial to her muscles. Perhaps, too, she felt that the bishop was watching her, and that made her a little nervous, for she could not help being aware that she was not handling the oars as well as when she started out. With a strong pull at her right oar to turn the boat inland, she got her left oar tangled between the water and the boat, so it seemed to her, and lost her hold of it. In a moment it was overboard and floating on the lake.

Leaning over the side of the boat, she made a grasp at the oar, but it was too far for her to reach it; and then, by a spasmodic movement of the other oar, the distance was increased.

The bishop's face grew pale. As he looked at her he saw that she was moving away from the floating oar, and now he understood why she had progressed so well. There was a considerable current in the lake which had carried her along, and was now moving the heavy boat much faster than it moved the oar. What should he tell her to do? If she could put her single oar out at the stern, she might scull the boat; but he was sure she did not understand sculling, and to try it she would have to stand up, and this would be madness.

She now took the other oar from the rowlock, and was about to rise, when the bishop shouted to her.

"What are you going to do?" he cried.

"I am going to the stern," she said, "to see if I cannot reach that oar with this one. Perhaps I can pull it in."

"For Heaven's sake, don't do that!" he cried. "Don't stand up, or the boat will tip, and you will fall overboard."

"But what can I do?" she called back. "I can't row with one oar."

"Try rowing a little on one side, and then on the other," said he. "Perhaps you can bring in the boat in that way."

She followed his suggestion, but very awkwardly, and he saw plainly that she was tired. Instead of approaching the shore, the boat continued to float down the lake.

Margery turned again. "Bishop," she cried, "what shall I do? I must do something, or I can't get ashore at all."

She did not look frightened; there was more of annoyance in her expression, as if she thought it impertinent in fate to treat her in this way, and she would not stand it.

"If I had thought of the current," said the bishop to himself, "I would never have let her go out alone, and she can't be trusted in that boat another minute longer. She will do something desperate." So saying, the bishop took off his hat and threw it on the ground. Then he unbuttoned his coat and began to take it off, but he suddenly changed his mind. Even in that

G

wilderness and under these circumstances he must appear respectable, so he buttoned his coat again, hastily took off his shoes, and, without hesitating, walked into the water until it was above his waist, and then calling to Margery that he was coming to her, he began to swim out into the lake. He did not strike out immediately for the boat, but directed his course towards the floating oar. Turning his head frequently towards Margery, he could see that she was sitting perfectly still, watching him, and so he kept on with a good heart.

The bishop was a powerful swimmer, but he found great difficulty in making his way through the water, on account of the extreme tightness of his clothes. It seemed to him that his arms and legs were bandaged in splints, as if he had been under a surgeon's care ; but still he struck out as well as he could, and in time reached the oar. Pushing this before him to the boat, Margery took hold of it.

"You swim splendidly," said she. "You can climb in right here."

But the bishop knew better than that, and worked his way round to the stern, and after holding on a little while to get his breath, he managed to clamber into the boat.

"Was the water very cold?" said she.

On his replying that it was, she said she thought so because he seemed stiff.

"Now, Miss Dearborn," said he, "I have made the stern seat very wet, but I don't believe you will mind that, and if you will sit here I will take the oars and row you in."

98

" BUT THE BISHOP KNEW BETTER "

"Oh, I think I can do that myself," said Margery. "I am rested now, and I am ever so much obliged to you for getting my oar for me."

Under almost any circumstances the bishop could smile, and now he smiled at the ridiculousness of the idea of Margery's rowing that boat back against the current, and with him in it.

"Indeed," said he, "I must insist. I shall freeze to death if I don't warm myself by exercise." So, reaching out his hand, he assisted Margery to the stern, and seating himself in her place, he took the oars, which she had drawn in.

"I don't see why I could not make the boat go along that way," said she, as they began to move steadily towards the camp. "I believe I could do it if people would only let me practise by myself; but they always want to show me how, and I hate to have anybody show me how. It is funny," she continued, "that you seem so very wet all but your collar. That looks as smooth and nice as if it had just come from the laundry."

The bishop laughed. "That is because it is gutta-percha," he said, "intended for rough use in camp; but the rest of my habiliments were not intended for wet weather."

"And you have no hat," said she. "Doesn't the sun hurt your head?"

"My head does feel a little warm," said he, "but I didn't want to row back to the place where I left my hat. It was not a good landing-place, after all. Besides," he said to himself, "I never thought of my hat or my shoes."

CHAPTER XII

WHEN the boat touched the shore Margery ran to the cabin to assure Mrs. Archibald of her safety, if she had been missed.

The bishop was sticking the stake in the hole from which he had pulled it, when Martin came running to him.

"That's a pretty piece of business!" cried the young man. "If you wanted to go out in the boat, why didn't you come to me for the key? You've got no right to pull up the stakes we've driven down. That's the same thing as stealing the boat. What's the matter? Did you tumble overboard? You must be a pretty sort of an oarsman! If the ladies want to go out in the boat, I am here to take them. I'd like you to understand that."

As has been said before, the bishop could smile under almost any circumstances, and he smiled now, but at the same time his brow wrinkled, which was not common when he smiled.

"I am going down to the shore to get my hat and shoes," he said, "and I would like you to come along with me. I can't stand here and talk to you."

"What do you want?" said Martin.

"Come along and see," said the bishop ; "that is, if you are not afraid."

That was enough, and the young man walked behind him until they reached the spot where the bishop had taken to the watcr. Then he stopped, and explained to Martin all that had happened.

"Now," said he, "what have you got to say?"

Martin, now that he knew that the bishop had plunged into the water for the sake of the beautiful Margery, was more jealously angry than when he had supposed he had merely taken her out to row.

"I haven't anything to say," he answered, shortly, "except that parsons had better attend to their own business, if they have any, and let young ladies and boats alone."

"Oh, that's all, is it?" said the bishop, and with a quick step forward he clutched the young man's arm with his right hand, while he seized his belt with the other, and then with a great heave sent him out into the water fully ten feet from the shore. With a splash like a dropped anchor Martin disappeared from view, but soon arose, his head and shoulders above the surface, where he stood for a moment, spluttering and winking and almost dazed.

The bishop stood on the bank and smiled. "Did you fall overboard?" said he. "You must be a pretty sort of a boatman!"

Without replying, Martin began to wade ashore.

"Come on," said the bishop ; "if you can't get up the bank, I'll help you."

But Martin needed no help ; he scrambled to

the bank, shook himself, and then advanced upon the bishop, fire in his eye and his fist clinched.

"Stop, young man," said the other. "It would not be fair to you if I did not tell you that I am a boxer and a heavy-weight, and that I threw you into the water because I didn't want to damage your face and eyes. You were impertinent, but I am satisfied, and the best thing you can do is to go and change your clothes before any one sees you in that plight. You are better off than I am, because I have no clothes with which to make a change." So saying, he sat down and began to put on his shoes.

Martin stood for a moment and looked at the bishop, he thought of Margery and a possible black eye, and then he walked as fast as he could to his tent to get some dry clothes. He was very wet, he was very hot, he was very angry, and what made him more angry than anything else was a respect for the bishop which was rising in him in spite of all his efforts to keep it down.

When Mr. Archibald and his party came back to camp late in the afternoon, Margery, who had already told her story to Mrs. Archibald, told it to each of the others. Mr. Archibald was greatly moved by the account of the bishop's bravery. He thoroughly appreciated the danger to which Margery had been exposed. There were doubtless persons who could be trusted so sit quietly in a little boat with only one oar, and to float upon a lake out of sight and sound of human beings until another boat could be secured and brought to the rescue, but Margery was not one of these persons. Her greatest danger had been

" WITH A GREAT HEAVE SENT HIM OUT INTO THE WATER "

that she was a child of impulse. He went immediately to Camp Roy to see the bishop and express his gratitude, for no matter how great the foolish good - nature of the man had been, his brave rescue of the girl was all that could be thought of now.

He found the bishop in bed, Mr. Clyde preparing the supper, and Mr. Raybold in a very bad humor.

"It's the best place for me," said the bishop, gayly, from under a heavy army blanket. "My bed is something like the carpets in Queen Elizabeth's time, and this shelter-tent is not one which can be called commodious, but I shall stay here until morning, and then I am sure I shall be none the worse for my dip into the cold lake."

As Mr. Archibald had seen the black garments of the bishop hanging on a bush as he approached the tent, he was not surprised to find their owner in bed.

"No," said the bishop, when Mr. Archibald had finished what he had to say, "there is nothing to thank me for. It was a stupid thing to launch a young girl out upon what, by some very natural bit of carelessness, might have become to her the waters of eternity, and it was my very commonplace duty to get her out of the danger into which I had placed her; so this, my dear sir, is really all there is to say about the matter."

Mr. Archibald differed with him for about ten minutes, and then returned to his camp.

Phil Matlack was also affected by the account of the rescue, and he expressed his feelings to Martin.

"He pulled up the stake, did he?" said Phil.

"Well, I'll make him pull up his stakes, and before he goes I've a mind to teach him not to meddle with other people's affairs."

"If I were you," said Martin, "I wouldn't try to teach him anything."

"You think he is too stupid to learn?" said Matlack, getting more and more angry at the bishop's impertinent and inexcusable conduct. "Well, I've taught stupid people before this."

"He's a bigger man than you are," said Martin.

Matlack withdrew the knife from the loaf of bread he was cutting, and looked at the young man.

"Bigger?" said he, scornfully. "What's that got to do with it? A load of hay is bigger than a crow-bar, but I guess the crow-bar would get through the hay without much trouble."

"You'd better talk about a load of rocks," said Martin. "I don't think you'd find it easy to get a crow-bar through them."

Matlack looked up inquiringly. "Has he been thrashing you?" he asked.

"No, he hasn't," said Martin, sharply.

"You didn't fight him, then?"

"No, I didn't," was the answer.

"Why didn't you? You were here to take charge of this camp and keep things in order. Why didn't you fight him?"

"I don't fight that sort of a man," said Martin, with an air which, if it were not disdainful, was intended to be.

Matlack gazed at him a moment in silence, and then went on cutting the bread. "I don't understand this thing," he said to himself. "I must look into it."

CHAPTER XIII

THE WORLD GOES WRONG WITH MR. RAYBOLD

THE next morning Mr. Archibald started out, very early, on a fishing expedition by himself. He was an enthusiastic angler, and had not greatly enjoyed the experience of the day before. He did not object to shooting if there were any legitimate game to shoot, and he liked to tramp through the mountain wilds under the guidance of such a man as Matlack ; but to keep company all day with Raybold, who, in the very heart of nature, talked only of the gossip of the town, and who punctuated his small talk by intermittent firing at everything which looked like a bird or suggested the movements of an animal, was not agreeable to him. Clyde was a better fellow, and Mr. Archibald liked him, but he was young and abstracted, and the interest which clings around an abstracted person who is young is often inconsiderable, so he determined for one day at least to leave Sir Cupid to his own devices, for he could not spend all his time defending Margery from amatory dawdle. For this one day he would leave the task to his wife.

That day Mr. Raybold was in a moody mood. Early in the morning he had walked to Sadler's, his object being to secure from the trunk which he had left there a suit of ordinary summer clothes. He had come to think that perhaps his bicycle attire, although very suitable for this sort of life, failed to make him as attractive in the eyes of youth and beauty as he might be if clothed in more becoming garments. It was the middle of the afternoon before he returned, and as he carried a large package, he went directly to his own camp, and in about half an hour afterwards he came over to Camp Rob dressed in a light suit, which improved his general appearance very much.

In his countenance, however, there was no improvement whatever, for he looked more out of humor than when he had set out, and when he saw that Mrs. Archibald was sitting alone in the shade, reading, and that at a considerable distance Harrison Clyde was seated by Margery, giving her a lesson in drawing upon birch bark, or else taking a lesson from her, his ill-humor increased.

"It is too bad," said he, taking a seat by Mrs. Archibald without being asked; "everything seems to go wrong out here in these woods. It is an unnatural way to live, anyhow, and I suppose it serves us right. When I went to Sadler's I found a letter from my sister Corona, who says she would like me to make arrangements for her to come here and camp with us for a time. Now that suits me very well indeed. My sister Corona is a very fine young woman, and I think it would be an excellent thing to have two young ladies here instead of one."

"Yes," said Mrs. Archibald, "that might be

very pleasant. I should be glad for Margery to have a companion of her own sex."

"I understand precisely," said Raybold, nodding his head sagaciously ; "of her own sex. Yes, I see your drift, and I agree with you absolutely. There is a little too much of that thing over there, and I don't wonder you are annoyed."

"I did not say I was annoyed," said Mrs. Archibald, rather surprised.

"No," he answered, "you did not say so, but I can read between the lines, even spoken lines. Now when I heard that my sister wanted to come out here," he continued, "at first I did not like it, for I thought she might be some sort of a restraint upon me ; but when I considered the matter further, I became very much in favor of it, and I sent a telegram by the stage telling her to come immediately, and that everything would be ready for her. My sister has a sufficient income of her own, and she likes to have everything suited to her needs. I am different. I am a man of the world, and although I do not always care to conform to circumstances, I can generally make circumstances conform to me. As Shakespeare says, 'The world is my pottle, and I stir my spoon.' You must excuse my quoting, but I cannot help it. My life work is to be upon the stage, and where one's mind is, there will his words be also."

Mr. Raybold was now in a much more pleasant mood than when he came to sit in the shade with Mrs. Archibald. He was talking ; he had found some one who listened and who had very little to say for herself.

"Consequently," he remarked, "I ordered from Mr. Sadler the very best tent that he had. It has two compartments in it, and it is really as comfortable as a house, and as my sister wrote that she wished a female attendant, not caring to have her meals cooked by boys—a very flippant expression, by-the-way—I have engaged for her a she-guide."

"A what?" asked Mrs. Archibald.

"A person," said he, "who is a guide of the female gender. She was the wife of a hunter who was accidentally shot, Sadler told me, by a young man who was with him on a gunning expedition. I told Sadler that it was reprehensible to allow such fellows to have guns, but he said that they are not as dangerous now as they used to be. This is because the guides have learned to beware of them, I suppose. This woman has lived in the woods and knows all about camp life, and Sadler says there could not be a better person found to attend a young lady in camp. So I engaged her, and I must say she charged just as much as if she were a man."

"Why shouldn't she," said Mrs. Archibald, "if she is just as good?"

To this remark Raybold paid no attention. "I will tell you," he said, "confidentially, of course, and I think you have as much reason to be interested in it as I have, why I came to view with so much favor my sister's coming here. She is a very attractive young woman, and I think she cannot fail to interest Clyde, and that, of course, will be of advantage to your niece."

"She is not my niece, you know," said Mrs. Archibald.

108

"Well," said he, "it is all the same. 'Let it be a bird wing or a flower, so it pleases'—a quotation which is also Avonian—and if Clyde likes Corona he will let Miss Dearborn alone. That's the sort of man he is."

"And in that case," said Mrs. Archibald, "I suppose you would not be unwilling to provide Margery with company."

"Madam," said the young man, leaning forward and fixing his eyes upon the ground, and then turning them upon her without moving his face towards her, "with me all that is a different matter. I may have occasion later to speak to you and your husband upon the subject of Miss Dearborn."

"In which case," said Mrs. Archibald, quickly, "I am sure that my husband will be very glad to speak to you. But why, may I ask, were you so disturbed when you came here, just now? You said the world was going wrong."

"I declare," said he, knitting his brows and clapping one hand on his knee, "I actually forgot! The world wrong? I should say it was wrong! My sister can't come, and I don't know what to do about it."

"Can't come?" asked Mrs. Archibald.

"Of course not," said he, all his ill-humor having returned. "That fellow, the bishop, is in our camp and in Clyde's bed. Clyde foolishly gave him his bed because he said the cook-tent was too cramped for a man to stay in it all day."

"Why need he stay?" asked Mrs. Archibald. "Has he taken cold? Is he sick?"

"No indeed," said Raybold. "If he were sick

we might send for a cart and have him taken to Sadler's, but the trouble is worse than that. His clothes, in which he foolishly jumped into the water, have shrunken so much that he cannot get them on, and as he has no others, he is obliged to stay in bed."

"But surely something can be done," said Mrs. Archibald.

"No," he interrupted, "nothing can be done. The clothes have dried, and if you could see them as they hang up on the bushes, you would understand why that man can never get into them again. The material is entirely unsuitable for out-door life. Clyde proposes that we shall lend him something, but there are no clothes in this party into which such a sausage of a man could get himself. So there he is, and there, I suppose, he will remain indefinitely; and I don't want to bring my sister to a camp with a permanently occupied hospital bed in it. As soon as I agreed to Corona's coming I determined to bounce that man, but now—" So saying, Mr. Raybold rose, folded his arms, and knit his brows, and as he did so he glanced towards the spot where Margery and Clyde had been sitting, and perceived that the latter had departed, probably to get some more birch bark; and so, with a nod to Mrs. Archibald, he sauntered away, bending his steps, as it were accidentally, in the direction of the young lady left alone.

When Mr. Archibald heard, that evening, of the bishop's plight and Raybold's discomfiture, he was amused, but also glad to know there was an opportunity for doing something practical for the bishop. He was beginning to like the man, in spite of his indefiniteness, so he went to see the bedridden prelate who was neither sick nor clerical, and with very little trouble induced him to take a few general measurements of his figure.

"It is so good of you," said the delighted recumbent, "that I shall not say a word, but step aside in deference to your conscience, whose encomiums will far transcend anything I can say. You will pardon me, I am sure, if I make my measurements liberal. The cost will not be increased, and to live, move, and breathe in a suit of clothes which is large enough for me is a joy which I have not known for a long time. Shoes, did you say, sir? Truly this is generosity supereminent."

"Yes," said Mr. Archibald, laughing, "and you also shall have a new hat. I will fit you out completely, and if this helps you to make a new and a good start in life, I shall be greatly gratified."

"Sir," said the bishop, the moisture of genuine gratitude in his eyes, "you are doing, I think, far more good than you can imagine, and pardon me if I suggest, since you are going to get me a hat, that it be not of clerical fashion. If everything is to be new, I should like everything different, and I am certain the cost will be less."

"All right," said Mr. Archibald. "I will now make a list of what you need, and I will write to one of my clerks, who will procure everything."

When Mr. Archibald went back to his camp he met Raybold, stalking moodily. Having been told what had been done for the bishop's relief, the young man was astonished.

"A complete outfit, and for him? I would not have dreamed of it; and besides, it is of no use; it must be days before the clothes arrive, and my sister wishes to come immediately."

"Do you suppose," exclaimed Mr. Archibald, "that I am doing this for the sake of your sister? I am doing it for the man himself."

When Mr. Archibald told his wife of this little interview they both laughed heartily.

"If Mr. Raybold's sister," said she, "is like him, I do not think we shall care to have her here; but sisters are often very different from their brothers. However, the bishop need not prevent her coming. If his clothes do not arrive before she does, I am sure there could be no objection to her tent being set up for a time in some of the open space in our camp, and then we shall become sooner acquainted with her; if she is a suitable person, I shall be very glad indeed for Margery to have a companion."

"All right," said Mr. Archibald; "let her pitch her tent where she pleases. I am satisfied."

CHAPTER XIV

IT was a week after her brother had sent her his telegram before Miss Corona Raybold arrived at Camp Rob, with her tent, her outfit, and her female guide. Mrs. Archibald had been surprised that she did not appear sooner, for, considering Mr. Raybold's state of mind, she had supposed that his sister had wished to come at the earliest possible moment.

"But," said Raybold, in explaining the delay, "Corona is very different from me. In my actions 'the thunder's roar doth crowd upon the lightning's heels,' as William has told us."

"Where in Shakespeare is that?" asked Mrs. Archibald.

Mr. Raybold bent his brow. "For the nonce," said he, "I do not recall the exact position of the lines." And after that he made no more Avonian quotations to Mrs. Archibald.

The arrival of the young lady was, of course, a very important event, and even Mr. Archibald rowed in from the lake when he saw her caravan approaching, herself walking in the lead. She proved to be a young person of medium height, slight, and dressed in a becoming suit of dark blue. Her hair and eyes were dark, her features

H   113

regular and of a classic cut, and she wore eye-glasses. Her manner was quiet, and at first she appeared reserved, but she soon showed that if she wished to speak she could talk very freely. She wore an air of dignified composure, but was affable, and very attentive to what was said to her.

Altogether she made in a short time an extreme-ly favorable impression upon Mr. and Mrs. Archi-bald, and in a very much less time an extremely unfavorable impression upon Margery.

Miss Raybold greeted everybody pleasantly, even informing Matlack that she had heard of him as a famous guide, and after thanking Mr. and Mrs. Archibald for their permission to set up her tent on the outskirts of their camp, she pro-ceeded to said tent, which was speedily made ready for her.

Mrs. Perkenpine, her guide, was an energetic woman, and under her orders the men who brought the baggage bestirred themselves wonderfully.

Just before supper, to which meal the Raybolds and Mr. Clyde had been invited, the latter came to Mr. Archibald, evidently much troubled and annoyed.

"I am positively ashamed to mention it to you, sir," he said, "but I must tell you that Raybold has ordered the men who brought his sister's tent to bring our tent over here and put it up near her's. I was away when this was done, and I wish to assure you most earnestly that I had nothing to do with it. The men have gone, and I don't suppose we can get it back to-night."

Mr. Archibald opened his eyes very wide.

"Your friend is certainly a remarkable young man," said he, "but we must not have any bad feeling in camp, so let everything remain as it is for to-night. I suppose he wished to be near his sister, but at least he might have asked permission."

"I think," said Clyde, "that he did not so much care to be near his sister as he did to be away from the bishop, who is now left alone in our little shelter-tent."

Mr. Archibald laughed. "Well," said he, "he will come to no harm, and we must see that he has some supper."

"Oh, I shall attend to that," said Clyde, "and to his breakfast also. And, now I come to think of it, I believe that one reason Raybold moved our tent over here was to get the benefit of his sister's cook. The bishop did our cooking, you know, before he took to his bed."

That evening Miss Raybold joined the party around the camp-fire. She declared that in the open air she did not in the least object to the use of tobacco, and then she asked Mr. Archibald if his two guides came to the camp-fire after their work was done.

"They do just as they please," was the answer. "Sometimes they come over here and smoke their pipes a little in the background, and sometimes they go off by themselves. We are very democratic here in camp, you know."

"I like that," said Miss Raybold, "and I will have Mrs. Perkenpine come over when she has arranged the tent for the night. Arthur, will you go and tell her?"

Her brother did not immediately rise to execute this commission. He hoped that Mr. Clyde would offer to do the service, but the latter did not improve the opportunity to make himself agreeable to the new-comer, and Raybold did the errand.

Harrison Clyde was sitting by Margery, and Margery was giving a little attention to what he said to her and a great deal of attention to Corona Raybold.

"More self-conceit and a better-fitting dress I never saw," thought Margery; "it's loose and easy, and yet it seems to fit perfectly, and I do believe she thinks she is some sort of an upper angel who has condescended to come down here just to see what common people are like."

Corona talked to Mr. Archibald. It was her custom always to talk to the principal personage of a party.

"It gives me pleasure, sir," said she, "to meet with you and your wife. It is so seldom that we find any one—" She was interrupted by Mrs. Perkenpine, who stood behind her.

The she-guide was a large woman, apparently taller than Matlack. Her sunburnt face was partly shaded by a man's straw hat, secured on her head by strings tied under her chin. She wore a very plain gown, coarse in texture, and of a light-blue color, which showed that it had been washed very often. Her voice and her shoes, the latter well displayed by her short skirt, creaked, but her gray eyes were bright, and moved about after the manner of searchlights.

"Well," said she to Miss Raybold, "what do you want?"

Corona turned her head and placidly gazed up at her. "I simply wished to let you know that you might join this company here if you liked. The two men guides are coming, you see."

Mrs. Perkenpine glanced around the group. "Is there any hunting stories to be told?" she asked.

Mr. Archibald laughed. "I don't know," he said, "but perhaps we may have some. I am sure that Matlack here has hunting stories to tell."

Mrs. Perkenpine shook her head. "No, sir," said she; "I don't want none of his stories. I've heard them all mostly two or three times over."

"I dare say you have," said Phil, seating himself on a fallen trunk, a little back from the fire; "but you see, Mrs. Perkenpine, you are so obstinate about keepin' on livin'. If you'd died when you was younger, you wouldn't have heard so many of those stories."

"There's been times," said she, "when you was tellin' the story of the bear cubs and the condensed milk, when I wished I had died when I was younger, or else you had."

"Perhaps," said Miss Raybold, in a clear, decisive voice, "Mr. Matlack may know hunting stories that will be new to all of us, but before he begins them I have something which I would like to say."

"All right," said Mrs. Perkenpine, seating herself promptly upon the ground; "if you're goin' to talk, I'll stay. I'd like to know what kind of things you do talk about when you talk."

"I was just now remarking," said Miss Corona, "that I am very glad indeed to meet with those who, like Mr. and Mrs. Archibald, are willing to set their feet upon the modern usages of society (which would crowd us together in a common herd) and assert their individuality."

Mr. Archibald looked at the speaker inquiringly.

"Of course," said she, "I refer to the fact that you and Mrs. Archibald are on a wedding-journey."

At this remark Phil Matlack rose suddenly from the tree-trunk and Martin dropped his pipe. Mr. Clyde turned his gaze upon Margery, who thereupon burst out laughing, and then he looked in amazement from Mr. Archibald to Mrs. Archibald and back again. Mrs. Perkenpine sat up very straight and leaned forward, her hands upon her knees.

"Is it them two sittin' over there?" she said, pointing to Margery and Clyde. "Are they on a honey-moon?"

"No!" exclaimed Arthur Raybold, in a loud, sharp voice. "What an absurdity! Corona, what are you talking about?"

To this his sister paid no attention whatever. "I think," she said, "it was a noble thing to do. An assertion of one's inner self is always noble, and when I heard of this assertion I wished very much to know the man and the woman who had so asserted themselves, and this was my principal reason for determining to come to this camp."

"But where on earth," asked Mr. Archibald, "did you hear that we were on a wedding-journey?"

"I read it in a newspaper," said Corona.

"I do declare," exclaimed Mrs. Archibald, "everything is in the newspapers! I did think that we might settle down here and enjoy ourselves without people talking about our reason for coming!"

"You don't mean to say," cried Mrs. Perkenpine, now on her feet, "that you two elderly ones is the honey-mooners?"

"Yes," said Mr. Archibald, looking with amusement on the astonished faces about him, "we truly are."

"Well," said the she-guide, seating herself, "if I'd stayed an old maid as long as that, I think I'd stuck it out. But perhaps you was a widow, mum?"

"No, indeed," cried Mr. Archibald; "she was a charming girl when I married her. But just let me tell you how the matter stands," and he proceeded to relate the facts of the case. "I thought," he said, in conclusion, turning to Matlack, "that perhaps you knew about it, for I told Mr. Sadler, and I supposed he might have mentioned it to you."

"No, sir," said Matlack, relighting his pipe, "he knows me better than that. If he'd called me and said, 'Phil, I want you to take charge of a couple that's goin' honey-moonin' about twenty-five years after they married, and a-doin' it for somebody else and not for themselves,' I'd said to him, 'They're lunatics, and I won't take charge of them.' And Peter he knows I would have thought that and would have said it, and so he did not mention the particulars to me. He knows that the only things that I'm afraid of in this world is lunatics. 'Tisn't only what they might do to me, but what they might do to themselves, and I won't touch 'em."

"I hope," said Mrs. Archibald, "that you don't consider us lunatics now that you have heard why we are here."

"Oh no," said the guide; "I've found that you're regular common-sense people, and I don't change my opinions even when I've heard particulars; but if I'd heard particulars first, it would have been all up with my takin' charge of you."

"And you knew it all the time?" said Clyde to Margery, speaking so that she only could hear.

"I knew it," she said, "but I didn't think it worth talking about. Do you know Mr. Raybold's sister? Do you like her?"

"I have met her," said Clyde; "but she is too lofty for me."

"What is there lofty about her?" said Margery.

"Well," said he, "she is lofty because she has elevated ideas. She goes in for reform; and for pretty much all kinds, from what I have heard."

"I think she is lofty," remarked Margery, "because she is stuck-up. I don't like her."

"It is so seldom," Corona now continued, "that we find people who are willing to assert their individuality, and when they are found I always want to talk to them. I suppose, Mr. Matlack, that your life is one long assertion of individuality?"

"What, ma'am?" asked the guide.

"I mean," said she, "that when you are out alone in the wild forest, holding in your hand the weapon which decides the question of life or death for any living creature over whom you may choose to exercise your jurisdiction, absolutely independent of every social trammel, every bond of conventionalism, you must feel that you are a predominant whole and not a mere integral part."

"Well," said Matlack, speaking slowly, "I may have had them feelin's, but if I did they must have struck in, and not come out on the skin, like measles, where I could see 'em."

"Corona," said her brother, in a peevish under-tone, "what is the good of all that? You're wasting your words on such a man."

His sister turned a mild steady gaze upon him. "I don't know any man but you," she said, "on whom I waste my words."

"Is assertin' like persistin'?" inquired Mrs. Perkenpine at this point.

"The two actions are somewhat alike," said Corona.

"Well, then," said the she-guide, "I'm in for assertin'. When my husband was alive there was a good many things I wanted to do, and when I wanted to do a thing or get a thing I kept on sayin' so; and one day, after I'd been keepin' on sayin' so a good while, he says to me, 'Jane,' says he, 'it seems to me that you're persistin'.' 'Yes,' says I, 'I am, and I intend to be.' 'Then you are goin' to keep on insistin' on persistin'?' says he. 'Yes,' says I; and then says he, 'If you keep on insistin' on persistin' I'll be thinkin' of 'listin'.' By which he meant goin' into the army as a regular, and gettin' rid of me; and as I didn't want to be rid of him, I stopped persistin'; but now I wish I had persisted, for then he'd 'listed, and most likely would be alive now, through not bein' shot in the back by a city fool with a gun."

"I do not believe," said Mrs. Archibald to her husband, when they had retired to their cabin, "that that young woman is going to be much of a companion for Margery. I think she will pre-fer your society to that of any of the rest of us. It is very plain that she thinks it is your individu-ality which has been asserted."

"Well," said he, rubbing his spectacles with his handkerchief before putting them away for the night, "don't let her project her individuality into my sport. That's all I have to say."

CHAPTER XV

A NET OF COBWEBS TO CAGE A LION

"I THINK there's something besides a lunatic that you are afraid of," said Martin to Matlack the next morning, as they were preparing breakfast.

"What's that?" inquired the guide, sharply.

"It's that fellow they call the bishop," said Martin. "He put a pretty heavy slur on you. You drove down a stake, and you locked your boat to it, and you walked away as big as if you were the sheriff of the county, and here he comes along, and snaps his fingers at you and your locks, and, as cool as a cucumber, he pulls up the stake and shoves out on the lake, all alone by herself, a young lady that you are paid to take care of and protect from danger."

"I want you to know, Martin Sanders," said Matlack, "that I don't pitch into a man when he's in his bed, no matter what it is that made him take to his bed or stay there. But I'll just say to you now, that when he gets up and shows himself, there'll be the biggest case of bounce in these parts that you ever saw."

"Bounce!" said Martin to himself, as he turned away. "I have heard so much of it lately that I'd like to see a little."

Matlack also communed with himself. "He's awful anxious to get up a quarrel between me and the parson," he thought. "I wonder if he was too free with his tongue and did get thrashed. He don't show no signs of it, except he's so concerned in his mind to see somebody do for the parson what he ain't able to do himself. But I'll find out about it! I'll thrash that fellow in black, and before I let him up I'll make him tell me what he did to Martin. I'd do a good deal to get hold of something that would take the conceit out of that fellow."

Mr. Arthur Raybold was a deep-minded person, and sometimes it was difficult for him, with the fathoming apparatus he had on hand, to discover the very bottom of his mind. Now, far below the surface, his thoughts revolved. He had come to the conclusion that he would marry Margery. In the first place, he was greatly attracted by her, and again he considered it would be a most advantageous union. She was charming to look upon, and her mind was so uncramped by conventionalities that it could adapt itself to almost any sphere to which she might direct it. He expected his life-work to be upon the stage, and what an actress Miss Dearborn would make if properly educated—as he could educate her! With this most important purpose in view, why should he waste his time? The Archibalds could not much longer remain in camp. They had limited their holiday to a month, and that was more than half gone. He must strike now.

The first thing to do was to get Clyde out of the way; then he would speak to Mr. Archibald and ask for authority to press his suit, and he would press that suit as few men on earth, he said to himself, would be able to press it. What girl could deny herself to him when he came to her clad not only with his own personal attributes, but with the fervor of a Romeo, the intellectuality of a Hamlet, and the force of an Othello?

The Clyde part of the affair seemed very simple ; as his party would of course have their own table Clyde would see his sister at every meal, and as Corona did not care to talk to him, and must talk to somebody, she would be compelled to talk to Clyde, and if she talked to Clyde and looked at him as she always did when she talked to people, he did not see how he could help being attracted by her, and when once that sort of thing began the Margery-field would be open to him.

He excused himself that morning for hurriedly leaving the breakfast-table by saying that he wished to see Mr. Archibald before he started out fishing.

He found that gentleman talking to Matlack. "Can I see you alone, sir?" said Raybold. "I have something of importance I wish to say to you."

"Very good," said the other, "for I have something I wish to say to you," and they retired towards the lake.

"What is it?" inquired Mr. Archibald.

"It is this," said Raybold, folding his arms as he spoke. "I am a man of but few words. When I have formed a purpose I call upon my actions to express it rather than my speech. I will not delay, therefore, to say to you that I love your ward, and my sole object in seeking this interview is to ask your permission to pay my addresses to her. That permission given, I will attend to the rest."

"After you have dropped your penny in the slot," remarked Mr. Archibald. "I must say," he continued, "that I am rather surprised at the nature of your communication. I supposed you were going to explain your somewhat remarkable conduct in bringing your tent into my camp without asking my permission or even speaking to me about it; but as what you have said is of so much more importance than that breach of good manners I will let the latter drop. But why did you ask my permission to address Miss Dearborn? Why didn't you go and do it just as you brought your tent here? Did you think that if you had a permit from me for that sort of sport you could warn off trespassers?"

"It was something of that kind," said Raybold, "although I should not have put it in that trifling way."

"Then I will remark," said Mr. Archibald, "that I know nothing of your matrimonial availability, and I do not want to know anything about it. My wife and I brought Miss Dearborn here to enjoy herself in the woods, not to be sought in marriage by strangers. For the present I am her guardian, and as such I say to you that I forbid you to make her a proposal of marriage, or, indeed, to pay her any attentions which she may consider serious. If I see that you do not respect

my wishes in this regard, I shall ask you to consider our acquaintance at an end, and shall dis-
pense with your visits to this camp. Have I
spoken plainly?"

The knitted brows of Raybold were directed
towards the ground. "You have spoken plainly,"
he said, "and I have heard," and with a bow he
walked away.

As he approached his tent a smile, intended to
be bitter, played about his features.

"A net of cobwebs," he muttered, "to cage a
lion!"

The weather had now grown sultry, the afternoon was very hot, and there was a general desire to lie in the shade and doze. Margery's
plans for a siesta were a little more complicated
than those of the others. She longed to lie in a
hammock under great trees, surrounded by the
leafy screens of the woodlands; to gaze at the
blue sky through the loop-holes in the towering
branches above her, and to dream of the mysteries
of the forest.

"Martin," said she, to the young guide, "is
there a hammock among the things we brought
with us?"

His face brightened. "Of course there are
hammocks," he said. "I wonder none of you
asked about them before."

"I never thought of it," said Margery. "I haven't
had time for lounging, and as for Aunt Harriet,
she would not get into one for five dollars."

"Where shall I hang it?" he asked.

"Not anywhere about here. Couldn't you find
some nice place in the woods, not far away, but

where I would not be seen, and might have a little time to myself? If you can, come and tell me quietly where it is."

"I know what she means," said Martin to himself. "It's a shame that she should be annoyed. I can find you just such a place," he said to Margery. "I will hang the hammock there, and I will take care that nobody else shall know where it is." And away he went, bounding heart and foot.

In less than a quarter of an hour he returned. "It's all ready, Miss Dearborn," he said. "I think I have found a place you will like. It's generally very close in the woods on a day like this, but there is a little bluff back of us, and at the end of it the woods are open, so that there is a good deal of air there."

"That is charming," said Margery, and with a book in her hand she accompanied Martin.

They were each so interested in the hammock business that they walked side by side, instead of one following the other, as had been their custom heretofore.

"Oh, this is a delightful place!" cried Margery. "I can lie here and look down into the very heart of the woods; it is a solitude like Robinson Crusoe's island."

"I am glad you like it," said Martin. "I thought you would. I have put up the hammock strongly, so that you need not be afraid of it; but if there is any other way you want it I can change it. There is not a thing here that can hurt you, and if a little snake should happen along it would be glad to get away from you if you give it a chance.

But if you should be frightened or should want anything you have only to call for me. I shall hear you, for I shall be out in the open just at the edge of the woods."

"Thank you very much," said Margery; "nothing could be nicer than this, and you did it so quickly."

He smiled with pleasure as he answered that he could have done it more quickly if it had been necessary ; and then he retired slowly, that she might call him back if she thought of anything she wanted.

Margery lay in the hammock, gazing out over the edge of the bluff into the heart of the woods ; her closed book was in her hand, and the gentle breeze that shook the leaves around her and disturbed the loose curls about her face was laden with a moist spiciness which made her believe it had been wandering through some fragrant foliage of a kind unknown to her, far away in the depths of the forest, where she could not walk on account of the rocks, the great bushes, and the tall ferns. It was lovely to lie and watch the leafy boughs, which seemed as if they were waving their handkerchiefs to the breeze as it passed.

"I don't believe," she said to herself, as she cast her eyes upward towards an open space above her, "that if I were that little white cloud and could float over the whole world and drop down on any spot I chose that I could drop into a lovelier place than this." Then she brought her gaze again to earth, and her mind went out between the shadowy trunks which stretched away and away and away towards the mysteries of the forest, which must always be mysteries to her because it was impossible for her to get to them and solve them—that is, if she remained awake. But if Master Morpheus should happen by, she might yet know everything—for there are no mysteries which cannot be solved in dreams.

Master Morpheus came, but with him came also Arthur Raybold; not by the little pathway that approached from the direction of the lake, but parting the bushes as if he had been exploring. When she heard footsteps behind her, Margery looked up quickly.

"Mr. Raybold!" she exclaimed. "How on earth did you happen here?"

"I did not happen," said he, wiping his brow with his handkerchief. "I have been looking for you, and I have had tough work of it. I saw you go into the woods, and I went in also, although some distance below here, and I have had a hard and tiresome job working my way up to you; but I have found you. I knew I should, for I had bent my mind to the undertaking."

"Well, I wish you hadn't," said Margery, in a vexed tone. "I came here to be alone and take a nap, and I wish you would find some other nice place and go and take a nap yourself."

He smiled deeply. "That would not answer my purpose at all," said he. "Napping is far from my desires."

"But I don't care anything about your desires," said Margery, in a tone which showed she was truly vexed, "I have pre-empted this place, and

I want it to myself. I was just falling into a
most delightful doze when you came, and I don't
think you have any right to come here and disturb
me."

"The sense of right, Miss Dearborn," said he,
"comes from the heart, and we do not have to
ask other people what it is. My heart has given
me the right to come here, and here I am."

"And what in the name of common-sense are
you here for?" said Margery. "Speaking about
your heart makes me think you came here to
make love to me. Is that it?"

"It is," said he, "and I wish you to hear me."

"Mr. Raybold," said she, her eyes as bright, he
thought, as if they had belonged to his sister
when she was urging some of her favorite views
upon a company, "I won't listen to one word of
such stuff. This is no place for love-making, and
I won't have it. If you want to make love to
me you can wait until I go home, and then you
can come and speak to my mother about it, and
when you have spoken to her you can speak to
me, but I won't listen to it here. Not one
word!"

Thus did the indignant craftiness of Margery
express itself. "It's a good deal better," she
thought, "than telling him no, and having him
keep on begging and begging."

"Miss Dearborn," said Raybold, "what I have
to say cannot be postponed. The words within
me must be spoken, and I came here to speak
them."

With a sudden supple twist Margery turned
herself, hammock and all, and stood on her feet

on the ground. "Martin!" she cried, at the top of her voice.

Raybold stepped back astonished. "What is this?" he exclaimed. "Am I to understand—"

Before he had time to complete his sentence Martin Sanders sprang into the scene.

"What is it?" he exclaimed, with a glare at Raybold, as if he suspected why he had been called.

"Martin," said Margery, with a good deal of sharpness in her voice, "I want you to take down this hammock and carry it away. I can't stay here any longer. I thought that at least one quiet place out-of-doors could be found where I would not be disturbed, but it seems there is no such place. Perhaps you can hang the hammock somewhere near our cabin."

Martin's face grew very red. "I think," said he, "that you ought not to be obliged to go away because you have been disturbed. Whoever disturbed you should go away, and not you."

Now Mr. Raybold's face also grew red. "There has been enough of this!" he exclaimed. "Guide, you can go where you came from. You are not wanted here. If Miss Dearborn wishes her hammock taken down, I will do it." Then turning to Margery, he continued: "You do not know what it is I have to say to you. If you do not hear me now, you will regret it all your life. Send this man away."

"I would very much like to send a man away if I knew how to do it," said Margery.

"Do it?" cried Martin. "Oh, Miss Dearborn, if you want it done, ask me to do it for you!" ·

"You!" shouted Raybold, making two steps towards the young guide; then he stopped, for Margery stood in front of him.

"I have never seen two men fight," said she, "and I don't say I wouldn't like it, just once; but you would have to have on boxing-gloves; I couldn't stand a fight with plain hands, so you needn't think of it. Martin, take down the hammock just as quickly as you can. And if you want to stay here, Mr. Raybold, you can stay, but if you want to talk, you can talk to the trees."

Martin heaved a sigh of disappointment, and proceeded to unfasten the hammock from the trees to which it had been tied. For a moment Raybold looked as if he were about to interfere, but there was something in the feverish agility of the young guide which made his close proximity as undesirable as that of a package of dynamite.

Margery turned to leave the place, but suddenly stopped. She would wait until Martin was ready to go with her. She would not leave those two young men alone.

Raybold was very angry. He knew well that such a chance for a private interview was not likely to occur again, and he would not give up. He approached the young girl.

"Margery," he said, "if you—"

"Martin," she cried to the guide, who was now ready to go, "put down that hammock and come here. Now, sir," she said, turning to Raybold, "let me hear you call me Margery again!"

She waited for about a half a minute, but she

was not called by name. Then she and Martin went away. She had nearly reached the cabin before she spoke, and then she turned to the young man and said: "Martin, you needn't trouble yourself about putting up that hammock now; I don't want to lie in it. I'm going into the house. I am very much obliged to you for the way you stood by me."

"Stood by you!" he exclaimed, in a low voice, which seemed struggling in the grasp of something which might or might not be stronger than itself. "You don't know how glad I am to stand by you, and how I would always—"

"Thank you," said Margery; "thank you very much," and she walked away towards the cabin.

"Oh, dear!" she sighed, as she opened the door and went in.

CHAPTER XVI

A MAN WHO FEELS HIMSELF A MAN

TOWARDS the end of the afternoon, when the air had grown cooler, Mr. Archibald proposed a boating expedition to the lower end of the lake. His boat was large enough for Matlack, the three ladies, and himself, and if the two young men wished to follow, they had a boat of their own.

When first asked to join the boating party Miss Corona Raybold hesitated ; she did not care very much about boating ; but when she found that if she stayed in camp she would have no one to talk to, she accepted the invitation.

Mr. Archibald took the oars nearest the stern, while Matlack seated himself forward, and this arrangement suited Miss Corona exactly.

The boat kept down the middle of the lake, greatly aided by the current, and Corona talked steadily to Mr. Archibald. Mrs. Archibald, who always wanted to do what was right, and who did not like to be left out of any conversation on important subjects, made now and then a re- mark, and whenever she spoke Corona turned to her and listened with the kindest attention, but the moment the elder lady had finished, the other resumed her own thread of observation without the slightest allusion to what she had just heard.

As for Mr. Archibald, he seldom said a word. He listened, sometimes his eyes twinkled, and he pulled easily and steadily. Doubtless he had a good many ideas, but none of them was expressed. As for Margery, she leaned back in the stern, and thought that, after all, she liked Miss Raybold better than she did her brother, for the young lady did not speak one word to her, nor did she appear to regard her in any way.

"But how on earth," thought Margery, "she can float over this beautiful water and under this lovely sky, with the grandeur of the forest all about her, and yet pay not the slightest attention to anything she sees, but keep steadily talking about her own affairs and the society she belongs to, I cannot imagine. She might as well live in a cellar and have pamphlets and reformers shoved down to her through the coal-hole."

Messrs. Clyde and Raybold accompanied the larger boat in their own skiff. It was an unwieldy craft, with but one pair of oars, and as the two young men were not accustomed to rowing together, and as Mr. Raybold was not accustomed to rowing at all and did not like it, Mr. Clyde pulled the boat. But, do what he could, it was impossible for him to get near the other boat. Matlack, who was not obliged to listen to Miss Corona, kept his eye upon the following skiff, and seemed to fear a collision if the two boats came close together, for if Clyde pulled hard he pulled harder. Arthur Raybold was not satisfied.

"I thought you were a better oarsman," he

said to the other ; "but now I suppose we shall not come near them until we land."

But the Archibald party did not land. Under the guidance of Matlack they swept slowly around the lower end of the lake ; they looked over the big untenanted camp - ground there ; they stopped for a moment to gaze into the rift in the forest through which ran the stream which connected this lake with another beyond it, and then they rowed homeward, keeping close to the farther shore, so as to avoid the strength of the current.

Clyde, who had not reached the end of the lake, now turned and determined to follow the tactics of the other boat and keep close to the shore, but on the side nearest to the camp. This exasperated Raybold.

"What are you trying to do?" he said. "If you keep in the middle we may get near them, and why should we be on one side of the lake and they on the other?"

"I want to get back as soon as they do," said Clyde, "and I don't want to pull against the current."

"Stop!" said Raybold. "If you are tired, let me have the oars."

Harrison Clyde looked for a minute at his companion, and then deliberately changed the course of the boat and rowed straight towards the shore, paying no attention whatever to the excited remonstrances of Raybold. He beached the boat at a rather poor landing-place among some bushes, and then, jumping out, he made her fast.

"What do you mean?" cried Raybold, as he

scrambled on shore. "Is she leaking more than she did? What is the matter?"

"She is not leaking more than usual," said the other, "but I am not going to pull against that current with you growling in the stern. I am going to walk back to camp."

In consequence of this resolution the two young men reached Camp Rob about the same time that the Archibald boat touched shore, and at least an hour before they would have arrived had they remained in their boat.

The party was met by Mrs. Perkenpine, bearing letters and newspapers. A man had arrived from Sadler's in their absence, and he had brought the mail. Nearly every one had letters; there was even something for Martin. Standing where they had landed, seated on bits of rock, on the grass, or on camp-chairs, all read their letters.

While thus engaged a gentleman approached the party from the direction of Camp Roy. He was tall, well built, handsomely dressed in a suit of light-brown tweed, and carried himself with a buoyant uprightness. A neat straw hat with a broad ribbon shaded his smooth-shaven face, which sparkled with cordial good-humor. A blue cravat was tied tastefully under a broad white collar, and in his hand he carried a hickory walking-stick, cut in the woods, but good enough for a city sidewalk. Margery was the first to raise her eyes at the sound of the quickly approaching footsteps.

"Goodness gracious!" she exclaimed, and then everybody looked up.

For a moment the new-comer was gazed upon

in silence. From what gigantic bandbox could this well-dressed stranger have dropped? Then, with a loud laugh, Mr. Archibald cried, "The bishop!"

No wonder there had not been instant recognition. The loose, easy-fitting clothes gave no hint of redundant plumpness; no soiled shovel-hat cast a shadow over the smiling face, and a glittering shirt front banished all thought of gutta-percha.

"Madam," exclaimed the bishop, raising his hat and stepping quickly towards Mrs. Archibald, "I cannot express the pleasure I feel in meeting you again. And as for you, sir," holding out his hand to Mr. Archibald, "I have no words in which to convey my feelings. Look upon a man, sir, who feels himself a man, and then remember from what you raised him. I can say no more now, but I can never forget what you have done," and as he spoke he pressed Mr. Archibald's hand with an honest fervor, which distorted for a moment the features of that gentleman.

From one to the other of the party the bishop glanced, as he said, "How glad, how unutterably glad, I am to be again among you!" Turning his eyes towards Miss Raybold, he stopped. That young lady had put down the letter she was reading, and was gazing at him through her spectacles with calm intensity. "This lady," said the bishop, turning towards Raybold, "is your sister, I presume? May I have the honor?"

Raybold looked at him without speaking. Here was an example of the silly absurdity of throwing pearls before swine. He had never wanted to have anything to do with the fellow when he was in the gutter, and he wanted nothing to do with him now.

With a little flush on her face Mrs. Archibald rose.

"Miss Raybold," she said, "let me present to you"—and she hesitated for a moment—"the gentleman we call the bishop. I think you have heard us speak of him."

"Yes," said Miss Raybold, rising, with a charming smile on her handsome face, and extending her hand, "I have heard of him, and I am very glad to meet him."

"I have also heard of you," said the bishop, as he stood smiling beside Corona's camp-chair, "and I have regretted that I have been the innocent means of preventing you for a time from occupying your brother's camp."

"Oh, do not mention that," said Corona, sweetly. "I walked over there yesterday, and I think it is a great deal pleasanter here, so you have really done me a favor. I am particularly glad to see you, because, from the little I have heard said about you, I think you must agree with some of my cherished opinions. For one thing, I am quite certain you favor the assertion of individuality; your actions prove that."

"Really," said the bishop, seating himself near her, "I have not given much thought to the subject; but I suppose I have asserted my individuality. If I have, however, I have done it indefinitely. Everybody about me having some definite purpose in life, and I having none, I am, in a negative way, a distinctive individual. It

is a pity I am so different from other people,
but—"

"No, it is not a pity," interrupted Corona, the
color coming into her checks and a brighter light
into her eyes. "Our individuality is a sacred responsibility. It is given to us for us to protect
and encourage — I may say, to revere. It is a
trust for which we should be called to account by
ourselves, and we shall be false and disloyal to
ourselves if we cannot show that we have done
everything in our power for the establishment
and recognition of our individuality."

"It delights me to hear you speak in that way,"
exclaimed the bishop. "It encourages and cheers
me. We are what we are; and if we can be
more fully what we are than we have been, then
we are more truly ourselves than before."

"And what can be nobler," cried Corona, "than
to be, in the most distinctive sense of the term,
ourselves?"

Mr. and Mrs. Archibald walked together towards their cabin.

"I want to be neighborly and hospitable," said
he, "but it seems to me that, now that the way
is clear for Miss Raybold to move her tent
to her own camp and set up house - keeping
there, we should not be called upon to enter-
tain her, and, if we want to enjoy ourselves in
our own way, we can do it without thinking of
her."

"We shall certainly not do it," said his wife,
"if we do think of her. I am very much disappointed in her. She is not a companion at all for
Margery; she never speaks to her; and, on the

other hand, I should think you would wish she would never speak to you."

"Well," said her husband, "that feeling did grow upon me somewhat this afternoon. Up to a certain point she is amusing."

Here he was interrupted by Mrs. Perkenpine, who planted herself before him.

"I s'pose you think I didn't do right," she said, "'cause, when that big bundle came it had your name on it; but I knew it was clothes, and that they was for that man in our camp, and so I took them to him myself. I heard Phil say that the sooner that man was up and dressed, the better it would be for all parties; and as Martin had gone off, and there wasn't nobody to take his clothes to him, I took them to him, and that's the long and short of it."

"I wondered how he got them," said Mr. Archibald, "but I am glad you carried them to him." Then, speaking to his wife, he added, "It may be a good thing that I gave him a chance to assert his individuality."

CHAPTER XVII

ABOUT half an hour after the beginning of the conversation between the bishop and Miss Corona, Mrs. Perkenpine came to the latter and informed her that supper was ready, and three times after that first announcement did she repeat the information. At last the bishop rose and said he would not keep Miss Raybold from her meal.

"Will you not join us?" she asked. "I shall be glad to have you do so."

The bishop hesitated for a moment, and then he accompanied Corona.

As Mrs. Perkenpine turned from the camp cooking-stove, a long-handled pan, well filled with slices of hot meat, in her hand, she stood for a moment amazed. Slowly approaching the little table outside of the tent were the bishop and Miss Raybold, and glancing beyond them towards the lake, she saw Clyde and Raybold, to whom she had yelled that supper was ready, the one with his arms folded, gazing out over the water, and the other strolling backward and forward, as if he had thought of going to his supper, but had not quite made up his mind to it.

Mrs. Perkenpine's face grew red. "They are waitin' for a chance to speak to that Archibald

143

gal," she thought. "Well, let them wait. And she's bringing him! She needn't s'pose I don't know him. I've seen him splittin' wood at Sadler's, and I don't cook for sech." So saying, she strode to some bushes a little back of the stove, and dashed the panful of meat behind them. Then she returned, and seizing the steaming coffee-pot, she poured its contents on the ground. Then she took up a smaller pan, containing some fried potatoes, hot and savory, and these she threw after the meat.

The bishop and Corona now reached the table and seated themselves. Mrs. Perkenpine, her face as hard and immovable as the trunk of an oak, approached, and placed before them some slices of cold bread, some butter, and two glasses of water.

Still earnestly talking, her eyes sometimes dimmed with tears of excitement as she descanted upon her favorite theories, Corona began to eat what was before her. She buttered a slice of bread, and if the bishop chanced to say anything she ate some of it. She drank some water, and she talked and talked and talked. She did not know what she was eating. It might have been a Lord Mayor's dinner or a beggar's crust; her mind took no cognizance of such an unimportant matter. As for her companion, he knew very well what he was eating, and as he gazed about him, and saw that there were no signs of anything more, his heart sank lower and lower; but he ate slice after slice of bread, for he was hungry, and he hoped that when the two young men came to the table they would call for more substantial food.

But long before they arrived Corona finished her meal and rose.

"Now that we have had our supper," she said, "let us go where we shall not be annoyed by the smell of food, and continue our conversation."

"Is it possible," thought the bishop, "that she can be annoyed by the smell of hot meat, potatoes, and coffee? I suppose the delicious odor comes from the other supper-table. Heavens! Why wasn't I asked there?"

There was a dreadful storm when Raybold and Clyde came to the table; but Mrs. Perkenpine remained hard and immovable through it all.

"Your sister and that tramp has been here," said she, "and this is all there is left. If you keep your hogs in your house, you can't expect to count on your victuals."

Some more coffee was made, and that, with bread, composed the young men's supper.

When Arthur Raybold had finished his meal, he walked to the spot where Corona and the bishop were conversing, and stood there silently. He was afraid to interrupt his sister by speaking to her, but he thought that his presence might have an effect upon her companion. It did have an effect, for the bishop seized the opportunity created by the arrival of a third party, excused himself, and departed at the first break in Corona's flow of words.

"I wish, Arthur," she said, "that when you see I am engaged in a conversation, you would wait at least a reasonable time before interrupting it."

"A reasonable time!" said Raybold, with a laugh. "I like that! But I came here to inter-

K   145

rupt your conversation. Do you know who that fellow is you were talking to? He's a common, good-for-nothing tramp. He goes round splitting wood for his meals. Clyde and I kept him here to cook our meals because we had no servant, and he's been in bed for days because he had no clothes to wear. Now you are treating him as if he were a gentleman, and you actually brought him to our table, where, like the half-starved cur that he is, he has eaten up everything fit to eat that we were to have for our supper."

"He did not eat all of it," said Corona, "for I ate some myself; and if he is the good-for-nothing tramp and the other things you call him, I wish I could meet with more such tramps. I tell you, Arthur, that if you were to spend the next five years in reading and studying, you could not get into your mind one-tenth of the serious information, the power to reason intelligently upon your perceptions, the ability to collate, compare, and refer to their individual causes the impressions—"

"Oh, bosh!" said her brother. "What I want to know is, are you going to make friends with that man and invite him to our table?"

"I shall invite him if I see fit," said she. "He is an extremely intelligent person."

"Well," answered he, "if you do I shall have a separate table," and he walked away.

As soon as he had left Corona, the bishop repaired to the Archibalds' cooking-tent, where he saw Matlack at work.

"I have come," he said, with a pleasant smile,

"to ask a very great favor. Would it be convenient for you to give me something to eat? Anything in the way of meat, hot or cold, and some tea or coffee, as I see there is a pot still steaming on your stove. I have had an unlucky experience. You know I have been preparing my own meals at the other camp, but to-day, when Mrs. Perkenpine brought me my clothes, she carried away with her all the provisions that had been left there. I supped, it is true, with Miss Raybold, but her appetite is so delicate and her fare so extremely simple that I confidentially acknowledge that I am half starved."

During these remarks Matlack had stood quietly gazing at the bishop. "Do you see that pile of logs and branches there?" said he; "that's the firewood that's got to be cut for to-morrow, which is Sunday, when we don't want to be cuttin' wood; and if you'll go to work and cut it into pieces to fit this stove, I'll give you your supper. You can go to the other camp and sleep where you have been sleepin', if you want to, and in the mornin' I'll give you your breakfast. I 'ain't got no right to give you Mr. Archibald's victuals, but what you eat I'll pay for out of my own pocket, considerin' that you'll do my work. Then to-morrow I'll give you just one hour after you've finished your breakfast to get out of this camp altogether, entirely out of my sight. I tried to have you sent away before, but other people took you up, and so I said no more; but now things are different. When a man pulls up what I've drove down, and sets loose what I've locked up, and the same as snaps his fingers in my face when

I'm attendin' to my business, then I don't let that man stay in my camp."

"Excuse me," said the bishop, "but in case I should not go away within the time specified, what would be your course?"

In a few brief remarks, inelegant but expressive, the guide outlined his intentions of taking measures which would utterly eliminate the physical energy of the other.

"I haven't taken no advantage of you," he said, "I haven't come down on you when you hadn't no clothes to go away in; and now that you've got good clothes, I don't want to spile them if I can help it; but they're not goin' to save you—mind my words. What I've said I'll stick to."

"Mr. Matlack," said the bishop, "I consider that you are entirely correct in all your positions. As to that unfortunate affair of the boat, I had intended coming to you and apologizing most sincerely for my share in it. It was an act of great foolishness, but that does not in the least excuse me. I apologize now, and beg that you will believe that I truly regret having interfered with your arrangements.

"That won't do!" exclaimed the guide. "When a man 'as much as snaps his fingers in my face, it's no use for him to come and apologize. That's not what I want."

"Nevertheless," said the bishop, "you will pardon me if I insist upon expressing my regrets. I do that for my own sake as well as yours; but we will drop that subject. When you ask me to cut wood to pay for my meals, you are entirely right, and I honor your sound opinion upon this subject. I will cut the wood and earn my meals, but there is one amendment to your plan which I would like to propose. To-morrow is Sunday; for that reason we should endeavor to make the day as quiet and peaceable as possible, and we should avoid everything which may be difficult of explanation or calculated to bring about an unpleasant difference of opinion among other members of the party. Therefore, will you postpone the time at which you will definitely urge my departure until Monday morning?"

"Well," said Matlack, "now I come to think of it, it might be well not to kick up a row on Sunday, and I will put it off until Monday morning; but mind, there's no nonsense about me. What I say I mean, and on Monday morning you march of your own accord, or I'll attend to the matter myself."

"Very good," said the bishop; "thank you very much. To-morrow I will consider your invitation to leave this place, and if you will come to Camp Roy about half-past six on Monday morning I will then give you my decision. Will that hour suit you?"

"All right," said Matlack, "you might as well make it a business matter. It's going to be business on my side, I'd have you know."

"Good — very good," said the bishop, "and now let me get at that wood."

So saying, he put down his cane, took off his hat, his coat, his waistcoat, his collar, and his cravat and his cuffs; he rolled up his sleeves, he turned up the bottoms of his trousers, and then taking an axe, he set to work.

In a few minutes Martin arrived on the scene. "What's up now?" said he.

"He's cuttin' wood for his meals," replied Matlack.

"I thought you were going to bounce him as soon as he got up?"

"That's put off until Monday morning," said Matlack. "Then he marches. I've settled that."

"Did he agree?" asked Martin.

"'Tain't necessary for him to agree; he'll find that out Monday morning."

Martin stood and looked at the bishop as he worked.

"I wish you would get him to cut wood every day," said he. "By George, how he makes that axe fly!"

When the bishop finished his work he drove his axe-head deep into a stump, washed his hands and his face, resumed the clothing he had laid aside, and then sat down to supper. There was nothing stingy about Matlack, and the wood-chopper made a meal which amply compensated him for the deficiencies of the Perkenpine repast.

When he had finished he hurried to the spot where the party was in the habit of assembling around the camp-fire. He found there some feebly burning logs, and Mr. Clyde, who sat alone, smoking his pipe.

"What is the matter?" asked the bishop. "Where are all our friends?"

"I suppose they are all in bed," said Clyde, "with the bedclothes pulled over their heads—

"" WHERE ARE ALL OUR FRIENDS ?""

that is, except one, and I suspect she is talking in her sleep. They were all here as usual, and Mr. Archibald thought he would break the spell by telling a fishing story. He told me he was going to try to speak against time; but it wasn't of any use. She just slid into the middle of his remarks as a duck slides into the water, and then she began an oration. I really believe she did not know that any one else was talking."

"That may have been the case," said the bishop; "she has a wonderful power of self-concentration."

"Very true," said Clyde, "and this time she concentrated herself so much upon herself that the rest of us got away, one by one, and when all the others had gone she went. Then, when I found she really had gone, I came back. By-the-way, bishop," he continued, "there is something I would like to do, and I want you to help me."

"Name it," said the other.

"I am getting tired of the way the Raybolds are trespassing on the good-nature of the Archibalds, and, whatever they do, I don't intend to let them make me trespass any longer. I haven't anything to do with Miss Raybold, but the other tent belongs as much to me as it does to her brother, and I am going to take it back to our own camp. And what is more, I am going to have my meals there. I don't want that woodenheaded Mrs. Perkenpine to cook for me."

"How would you like me to do it?" asked the bishop, quickly.

"That would be fine," said Clyde. "I will help, and we will set up house-keeping there again, and if Raybold doesn't choose to come and live in his own camp he can go wherever he pleases. I am not going to have him manage things for me. Don't you think that you and I can carry that tent over?"

"With ease!" exclaimed the bishop. "When do you want to move—Monday morning?"

"Yes," said Clyde, "after breakfast."

CHAPTER XVIII

DURING the next day no one in camp had reason to complain of Corona Raybold. She did not seem inclined to talk to anybody, but spent the most of her time alone. She wrote a little and reflected a great deal, sometimes walking, sometimes seated in the shade, gazing far beyond the sky.

When the evening fire was lighted, her mood changed so that one might have supposed that another fire had been lighted somewhere in the interior of her mental organism. Her fine eyes glistened, her cheeks gently reddened, and her whole body became animated with an energy created by warm emotions.

" I have something I wish to say to you all," she exclaimed, as she reached the fire. " Where is Arthur? Will somebody please call him? And I would like to see both the guides. It is something very important that I have to say. Mrs. Perkenpine will be here in a moment ; I asked her to come. If Mr. Matlack is not quite ready, can he not postpone what he is doing? I am sure you will all be interested in what I have to say, and I do not want to begin until every one is here."

Mr. Archibald saw that she was very much in earnest, and so he sent for the guides, and Clyde went to call Raybold.

In a few minutes Clyde returned and told Corona that her brother had said he did not care to attend services that evening.

"Where is he?" asked Miss Raybold.

"He is sitting over there looking out upon the lake," replied Clyde.

"I will be back almost immediately," said she to Mr. Archibald, "and in the mean time please let everybody assemble."

Arthur Raybold was in no mood to attend services of any sort. He had spent nearly the whole day trying to get a chance to speak to Margery, but never could he find her alone.

"If I can once put the matter plainly to her," he said to himself, "she will quickly perceive what it is that I offer her; and when she clearly sees that, I will undertake to make her accept it. She is only a woman, and can no more withstand me than a mound of sand built by a baby's hand could withstand the rolling wave."

At this moment Corona arrived and told him that she wanted him at the camp-fire. He was only a man, and could no more withstand her than a mound of sand built by a baby's hand could withstand the rolling wave.

When everybody in the camp had gathered around the fire, Corona, her eye-glasses illumined by the light of her soul, gazed around the circle and began to speak.

"My dear friends," she said, "I have been thinking a great deal to-day upon a very important subject, and I have come to the conclusion that we who form this little company have before us one of the grandest opportunities ever afforded a group of human beings. We are here, apart from our ordinary circumstances and avocations, free from all the trammels and demands of society, alone with nature and ourselves. In our ordinary lives, surrounded by our ordinary circumstances, we cannot be truly ourselves; each of us is but part of a whole, and very often an entirely unharmonious part. It is very seldom that we are able to do the things we wish to do in the manner and at times and places when it would best suit our natures. Try as we may to be true to ourselves, it is seldom possible; we are swept away in a current of conventionality. It may be one kind of conventionality for some of us and another kind for others, but we are borne on by it all the same. Sometimes a person like myself or Mr. Archibald clings to some rock or point upon the bank, and for a little while is free from the coercion of circumstances, but this cannot be for long, and we are soon swept with the rest into the ocean of conglomerate commonplace."

"That's when we die !" remarked Mrs. Perkenpine, who sat reverently listening.

"No," said the speaker, "it happens while we are alive. But now," she continued, "we have a chance, as I said before, to shake ourselves free from our enthralment. For a little while each one of us may assert his or her individuality. We are a varied and representative party ; we come from different walks of life ; we are men, women, and—" looking at Margery, she was about to say children, but she changed her expression to "young people." "I think you will all understand what I mean. When we are at our homes we do things because other people want us to do them, and not because we want to do them. A family sits down to a meal, and some of them like what is on the table, some do not ; some of them would have preferred to eat an hour before, some of them would prefer to eat an hour later ; but they all take their meals at the same time and eat the same things because it is the custom to do so.

"I mention a meal simply as an instance, but the slavery of custom extends into every branch of our lives. We get up, we go to bed, we read, we work, we play, just as other people do these things, and not as we ourselves would do them if we planned our own lives. Now we have a chance, all of us, to be ourselves ! Each of us may say, 'I am myself, one !' Think of that, my friends, each one ! Each of us a unit, responsible only to his or her unity, if I may so express it."

"Do you mean that I am that ?" inquired Mrs. Perkenpine.

"Oh yes," replied Corona.

"Is Phil Matlack one ?"

"Yes."

"All right," said the female guide ; "if he is one, I don't mind."

"Now what I propose is this," said Corona : "I understand that the stay in this camp will continue for about a week longer, and I earnestly urge upon you that for this time we shall each one of us assert our individuality. Let us be what we are, show ourselves what we are, and let each other see what we are."

"It would not be safe nor pleasant to allow everybody to do that," said Mr. Archibald. He was more interested in Miss Raybold's present discourse than he had been in any other he had heard her deliver.

"Of course," said she, "it would not do to propose such a thing to the criminal classes or to people of evil inclinations, but I have carefully considered the whole subject as it relates to us, and I think we are a party singularly well calculated to become the exponent of the distinctiveness of our several existences."

"That gits me," said Matlack.

"I am afraid," said the speaker, gazing kindly at him, "that I do not always express myself plainly to the general comprehension, but what I mean is this : that during the time we stay here, let each one of us do exactly what he or she wants to do, without considering other people at all, except, of course, that we must not do anything which would interfere with any of the others doing what they please. For instance—and I assure you I have thought over this matter in all its details—if any of us were inclined to swear or behave disorderly, which I am sure could not be the case, he or she would not do so because he or she would feel that, being responsible to himself or herself, that responsibility would prevent him or her from doing that which would interfere with the pleasure or comfort of his or her associates."

"I think," said Mrs. Archibald, somewhat severely, "that our duty to our fellow-beings is far more important than our selfish consideration of ourselves."

"But reflect," cried Corona, "how much consideration we give to our fellow-beings, and how little to ourselves as ourselves, each one. Can we not, for the sake of knowing ourselves and honoring ourselves, give ourselves to ourselves for a little while? The rest of our lives may then be given to others and the world."

"I hardly believe," said Mr. Archibald, "that all of us clearly understand your meaning, but it seems to me that you would like each one of us to become, for a time, a hermit. I do not know of any other class of persons who so thoroughly assert their individuality."

"You are right!" exclaimed Corona. "A hermit does it. A hermit is more truly himself than any other man. He may dwell in a cave and eat water-cresses, he may live on top of a tall pillar, or he may make his habitation in a barrel! If a hermit should so choose, he might furnish a cave with Eastern rugs and bric-à-brac. If he liked that sort of thing, he would be himself. Yes, I would have all of us, in the truest sense of the word, hermits, each a hermit; but we need not dwell apart. Some of us would certainly wish to assert our individuality by not dwelling apart from others."

"We might, then," said Mr. Archibald, "become a company of associate hermits."

"Exactly!" cried Corona, stretching out her hands. "That is the very word—associate hermits. My dear friends, from to-morrow morning, until we leave here, let us be associate hermits. Let us live for ourselves, be true to ourselves. After all, if we think of it seriously, ourselves are all that we have in this world. Everything else may be taken from us, but no one can take from me, myself, or from any one of you, yourself."

The bishop now rose. He as well as the others had listened attentively to everything that had been said; even Arthur Raybold had shown a great deal of interest in his sister's remarks.

"You mean," said the bishop, "that while we stay here each one of us shall act exactly as we think we ought to act if we were not influenced by the opinions and examples of others around us, and thus we shall have an opportunity to find out for ourselves and show others exactly what we are."

"That is it," said Corona, "you have stated it very well."

"Well, then," said the bishop, "I move that for the time stated we individually assert our individuality."

"Second the motion," said Mr. Archibald.

"All in favor of this motion please say 'Aye,'" said Corona. "Now let everybody vote, and I hope you will all say 'Aye,' and if any one does not understand, I will be happy to explain."

"I want to know," said Phil Matlack, rising, "if one man asserts what you call his individ'ality in such a way that it runs up agin another man's, and that second man ain't inclined to stand it, if that—"

"Oh, I assure you," interrupted the bishop,

"that that will be all right. I understand you perfectly, and the individualities will all run along together without interfering with each other, and if one happens to get in the way of another it will be gently moved aside."

"Gently !" said Matlack, somewhat satirically. "Well, all right, it will be moved aside. I am satisfied, if the rest are."

" Now all in favor say 'Aye,'" said Corona.

They all said "Aye," except Mrs. Perkenpine, who said " Me."

VERY early the next morning Margery pushed wide open the window of her studio chamber. The sash was a large one, and opened outward on hinges. She looked out upon the dewy foliage, she inhaled the fragrance of the moist morning air, she listened to the song of some early birds, and then, being dressed for the day, she got on a chair, stepped on the window-sill, and jumped out. She walked quietly round the cabin and went out towards the lake. She had never seen the woods so early in the day. All the space between the earth and the sky seemed filled with an intoxicating coolness. She took off her hat and carried it in her hand ; the sun was not yet high enough to make it necessary to put anything between him and her.

" This is what I am," said Margery to herself as she stepped blithely on. " I never knew before what I am. I am really a dryad under difficulties."

Presently, to her amazement and his amazement, she saw Martin. She went towards him.

" Oh, Martin," she said, " are you up so early ?"

He smiled. " This is not early for me," he answered.

"And Mr. Matlack, is he up?"

"Oh yes, he is up, and gone off to attend to some business."

"Well, really!" exclaimed Margery. "I thought I was the first one out in the world to-day. And now, Martin, don't you want to do something for me? I did not think it would happen, but I am really dreadfully hungry, and couldn't you give me my breakfast now, by myself, before anybody else? I am not particular what I have—anything that is easy to get ready will do—and I would like it down at the very edge of the lake."

"You shall have it!" exclaimed Martin, eagerly. "I will get it ready for you very soon, and will bring it to you. I know you like bread and butter and jam, and there is some cold meat, and I will boil you an egg and make some coffee."

"That will be lovely," said Margery, "and I will go down by the lake and wait. I do believe," she said to herself as she hurried away, "that this hermit business is the only sensible thing that ever came into the head of that classic statue with the glass fronts."

Very soon Martin appeared with a rug, which he said she would want if she were going to sit on the ground; and then he ran away, but soon came back with the breakfast. Margery was surprised to see how tastefully it was served.

"You could not have done it better," she said, "if you had been a"—she was about to say waiter, but as she gazed at the bright, handsome face of the young man she felt that it would hurt his feelings to use such a word, so she suddenly changed it to woman.

162

"If it is done well," he said, "it is not because I am like a woman, but because you are one."

"What does that mean?" thought Margery; but she did not stop to consider. "Thank you very much," she said. "Here is where I am going to eat, and nobody will disturb me."

"Do you wish anything else?" he asked.

"No," said she. "I have everything I want; you know I take only one cup of coffee."

He did know it; he knew everything she took, and as he felt that there was no excuse for him to stay there any longer, he slowly walked away.

The place Margery had chosen was a nice little nook for a nice little hermit. It was a bit of low beach, very narrow, and flanked on the shore side by a row of bushes, which soon turned and grew down to the water's edge, thus completely cutting off one end of the beach. At the other end the distance between the shrubbery and the water was but a few feet, so that Margery could eat her breakfast without being disturbed by the rest of the world.

Reclining on the rug with the little tray on the ground before her, and some green leaves and a few pale wild flowers peeping over the edge of it to see what she had for breakfast, Margery gave herself up to the enjoyment of life.

"Each, one," she said aloud; "I am one, and beautiful nature is another. Just two of us, and each, one. Go away, sir," she said to a big buzzing creature with transparent wings, "you are another, but you don't count."

Arthur Raybold was perhaps the member of the party who was the best satisfied to be himself.

He had vowed, as he left the camp-fire the night before, that his sister had at last evolved an idea which had some value. Be himself? He should think so! He firmly believed that he was the only person in the camp capable of truly acting his own part in life.

Clyde had told him that on this morning he was going to move the tent over to their own camp, and though he had objected very forcibly, he found that Clyde was not to be moved, and that the tent would be. In an angry mood he had been the first one of the Associated Hermits to assert his individuality. He made up his mind that he would not leave the immediate atmosphere of Margery. He would revolve about her in his waking hours and in his dreams, and in the latter case he would revolve in a hammock hung between two trees not far from his sister's tent; and as he was not one who delayed the execution of his plans, he had put up the hammock that night, although his tent was still in Camp Rob. He had not slept very well, because he was not used to repose in a hammock; and he had risen early, for, though wrapped in a blanket, he had had found himself a little chilly.

Starting out for a brisk walk to warm himself, he had not gone far before he thought he heard something which sounded like the clicking of knife and fork and dish. He stopped, listened, and then approached the source of the sounds, and soon stood at the open end of Margery's little beach. For a few moments she did not know he was there, so engrossed was her mind with the far-away shadows on the lake, and with the piece of bread and jam she held in her hand.

"Oh, happy Fates !" he exclaimed. "How have ye befriended me ! Could I have believed such rare fortune was in store for me ?"

At the sound of his voice Margery turned her head and started, and in the same instant she was on her feet.

"Margery," he said, without approaching her, but extending his arms so that one hand touched the bushes and the other reached over the water, "I have you a gentle prisoner. I consider this the most fortunate hour of my whole existence. All I ask of you is to listen to me for ten minutes, and then I will cease to stand guard at the entrance to your little haven, and although you will be free to go where you please, I know you will not go away from me."

Margery's face was on fire. She was so angry she could scarcely speak, but she managed to bring some words to her lips to express her condition of mind.

"Mr. Raybold," she cried, "if I ever hear any more of that horrid trash from you I will speak to Mr. Archibald, and have him drive you out of this camp. I haven't spoken to him before because I thought it would make trouble and interfere with people who have not done anything but what is perfectly right, but this is the last time I am going to let you off, and I would like you to remember that. Now go away this instant, or else step aside and let me pass."

Raybold did not change his position, but with a smile of indulgent condescension he remarked :

"Now, then, you are angry ; but I don't mind that, and I am quite sure you do not mean it. You see, you have never heard all that I have to say to you. When I have fully spoken to you, then I have no fear—"

He had not finished his sentence, when Margery dashed into the water, utterly regardless of her clothes, and before the astonished intruder could advance towards her she had rushed past him, and had run up on dry land a yard or two behind him. The water on the shelving beach was not more than a foot deep, but her mad bounds made a splashing and a spattering of spray as if a live shark had been dropped into the shallow water. In a moment she had left the beach and was face to face with Martin, pale with fright.

"I thought you had tumbled in !" he cried. "What on earth is the matter ?"

She had no breath to answer, but she turned her head towards the lake, and as Martin looked that way he saw Raybold advancing from behind the bushes. It required no appreciable time for the young guide to understand the situation. His whole form quivered, his hands involuntarily clinched, his brows knitted, and he made one quick step forward ; but only one, for Margery seized him by the wrist. Without knowing what he was doing, he struggled to free himself from her, but she was strong and held him fast.

"I must go to my tent," she gasped. "I am all wet. Now promise me that you will not say a thing or do a thing until I see you again. Promise !"

For a moment he seemed undecided, and then

he ceased his efforts to get away, and said, "I promise."

Margery dropped his arm and hurried towards the cabin, hoping earnestly that the Archibalds were not yet up.

"This is a gay and lively beginning for a hermit," she thought, as she made her way around the house, "and I don't see how on earth I am ever going to get through that window again. There is nothing to stand on. I did not expect to go back until they were all up."

But when she reached the window there was a stout wooden stool placed below it.

"Martin did that," she thought, "while I was at my breakfast. He knew I must have come through the window, and might want to go back that way. Oh dear!" she sighed. "But I am sure I can't help it." And so, mounting from the stool to the window-sill, she entered her room.

Having given his promise, Martin turned his back upon the sombre young man, who, with folded arms and clouded brow, was stalking towards the tents at the other end of the camp.

"If I look at him," said Martin, "it may be that I could not keep my promise."

It was about half an hour afterwards, when Martin, still excited and still pale, was getting ready for the general breakfast, forgetting entirely that he was a hermit, and that some of the other hermits might have peculiar ideas about their morning meal, that Phil Matlack arrived on the scene. Martin was very much engrossed in his own thoughts, but he could not repress an inquiring interest in his companion.

"Well," said he, "did you bounce him?"

Matlack made no answer, but began to cut out the top of a tin can.

"I say," repeated Martin, "did you bounce him, or did he go without it?"

Without turning towards the younger man, Matlack remarked: "I was mistaken. That ain't fat; it's muscle."

"You don't mean to say," exclaimed Martin, in astonishment, "that he bounced you out of that camp!"

"I don't mean to say nothin'," was the reply, "except what I do say; and what I say is that that ain't fat; it's muscle. When I make a mistake I don't mind standin' up and sayin' so."

Martin could not understand the situation. He knew Matlack to be a man of great courage and strength, and one who, if he should engage in a personal conflict, would not give up until he had done his very best. But the guide's appearance gave no signs of any struggle. His clothes were in their usual order, and his countenance was quiet and composed.

"Look here," cried Martin, "how did you find out all that about the bishop?"

Matlack turned on him with a grim smile. "Didn't you tell me that day you was talkin' to me about the boat that he was a tough sort of a fellow?"

"Yes, I did," said the other.

"Well," said Matlack, "how did you find that out?"

Martin laughed. "I shouldn't wonder," he said, "if we were about square. Well, if you will tell me how you found it out, I will tell you how I did."

"Go ahead," said the other.

"The long and short of my business with him," said Martin, "was this : I went with him down to the lake, and there I gave him a piece of my mind ; and when I had finished, he turned on me and grabbed me with his two hands and chucked me out into the water, just as if I had been a bag of bad meal that he wanted to get rid of. When I got out I was going to fight him, but he advised me not to, and when I took a look at him and remembered the feel of the swing he gave me, I took his advice. Now what did he do to you ?"

"He didn't do nothin'," said Matlack. "When I got to the little tent he sleeps in, there he was sittin' in front of it, as smilin' as a basket of chips, and he bade me good-mornin' as if I had been a tenant comin' to pay him his rent ; and then he said that before we went on with the business between us, there was some things he would like to show me, and he had 'em all ready. So he steps off to a place a little behind the tent, and there was three great bowlders, whopping big stones, which he said he had brought out of the woods. I could hardly believe him, but there they was. 'You don't mean,' says I, 'that you are goin' to fight with stones ; because, if you are, you ought to give me a chance to get some,' and I thought to myself that I would pick up rocks that could be heaved. 'Oh no,' says he, with one of them smiles of his—'oh no ; I just want to open our conference with a little gymnastic exhibition.' And so sayin', he rolled up his shirt-sleeves—he hadn't no coat on—and he picked up one of them rocks with both hands, and then he gave it a swing with one hand, like you swing a ten-pin ball, and he sent that rock about thirty feet.

"It nearly took my breath away, for if I had to move such a stone I'd want a wheelbarrow. Then he took another of the rocks and hurled it right on top of the first one, and it came down so hard that it split itself in half. And then he took up the third one, which was the biggest, and threw it nearly as far, but it didn't hit the others. 'Now, Mr. Matlack,' says he, 'this is the first part of my little programme. I have only one or two more things, and I don't want to keep you long.' Then he went and got a hickory sapling that he'd cut down. It was just the trunk part of it, and must have been at least three inches thick. He put the middle of it at the back of his neck, and then he took hold of the two ends with his hands and pulled forward, and, by George! he broke that stick right in half!

"Then says he, 'Would you mind steppin' down to the lake?' I didn't mind, and went with him, and when we got down to the water there was their boat drawed up on the shore and pretty nigh full of water. 'Mr. Clyde brought this boat back the other day,' says he, 'from a place where he left it some distance down the lake, and I wonder he didn't sink before he got here. We must try and calk up some of the open seams; but first we've got to get the water out of her.' So sayin', he squatted down on the ground in front of the boat and took hold of it, one hand on one side of the bow and one on the

other, and then he gave a big twist, and just
turned the boat clean over, water and all, so that
it lay with its bottom up, and the water running
down into the lake like a little deluge.

" 'That ought to have been done long ago,' says
he, 'and I'll come down after a while and calk it
before the sun gets on it.' Then he walked back
to camp as spry as a robin, and then says he, 'Mr.
Matlack, my little exhibition is over, and so we'll
go ahead with the business you proposed.' I
looked around, and says I : 'Do you find that
little tent you sleep in comfortable? It seems to
me as if your feet must stick out of it.' 'They
do,' says he, 'and I sometimes throw a blanket
over them to keep them dry. But we are goin'
to make different arrangements here. Mr. Clyde
and I will bring down his tent after breakfast,
and if Mr. Raybold doesn't choose to occupy it,
Mr. Clyde says I may share it with him. At any
rate, I've engaged to attend to the cookin' and to
things in general in this camp durin' the rest of
the time we stay here.'

" 'And so Mr. Clyde is tired of trespassin', is
he?' says I. 'Yes, he is,' says he ; 'he's a high-
minded young fellow, and doesn't fancy that sort
of thing. Mr. Raybold slept last night in a hammock, and if that suits him, he may keep it up.'
'If I was you,' says I, 'if he does come back to
the camp, I'd make him sleep in that little tent.
It would fit him better than it does you.' 'Oh
no,' says he, 'I don't want to make no trouble.
I'm willin' to sleep anywhere. I'm used to rough-
in' it, and I could make myself comfortable in any
tent I ever saw.' 'Well,' says I, 'that was a very

171

pretty exhibition you gave me, and I am much obliged to you, but I must be goin' over to my camp to help get breakfast.' 'If you see Mr. Clyde,' says he, 'will you kindly tell him that I will come over and help him with his tent in about an hour?' To which I said I would, and I left. Now then, hurry up. Them hermits will want their breakfasts."

CHAPTER XX

MARTIN ASSERTS HIS INDIVIDUALITY

"Good - morning," said Mr. Clyde, as he approached Mr. and Mrs. Archibald, seated opposite each other at their breakfast-table. "So you still eat together? Don't ask me to join you; I have had my breakfast."

"Yes," said Mr. Archibald, "we did think that, as we were hermits, we ought to eat in some separate, out-of-the-way fashion; but we could not think of any, and as we were both hungry and liked the same things, we concluded to postpone the assertion of our individualities."

"And Miss Dearborn?" asked Clyde.

"Oh, she had her breakfast long ago, so she told us," said Mrs. Archibald. "I suppose she took some bread and jam, for I do not know what else she could have had."

"As for me," said Clyde, "I thought I would do something of the sort. I like an early breakfast, and so I turned out, more than an hour ago and went to look up Mrs. Perkenpine; and I might as well say, sir, that I am now looking for the bishop to come and help me carry our tent back to our own camp, where he is going to cook for us. I never wanted to be a trespasser on your premises, and I don't intend to be such any longer."

"That's the right feeling," said Mr. Archibald; "although, in fact, it doesn't make any difference to us whether your party camps here or not. At first I thought it would, but I find it does not."

"By which he means," said Mrs. Archibald, "that if you want to go away he is perfectly willing to have you stay, but if you don't want to go away he doesn't like it, and would have you move."

Clyde laughed. "I haven't anything to say for the others," he answered, "but as long as I have a camp of my own I think I ought to live there."

"But how about Mrs. Perkenpine?" asked Mrs. Archibald. "Did you find her willing to wait on you, one at a time?"

"Not exactly," said Clyde. "I discovered her, by her kitchen tent, hard at work eating her own breakfast. I must have looked surprised, for she lost no time in telling me that she was a hermit, and was living for one person at a time—herself first—and that she was mighty glad to get a chance to have her breakfast before anybody else, for she was always hungry and hated waiting. I looked at the table, and saw that she had the breakfast ready for the whole party; so I said, 'I am a hermit too, and I am living for myself, and so I am going to sit down and eat.' 'Squat,' said she, and down I sat; and I had the best meal of her cooking that I have yet tasted. I told her so, and she said she shouldn't wonder. 'Because,' said she, 'I cooked this breakfast for myself—me, one—and as I wasn't thinkin' what other people 'd like, I got things a little more tasty than common, I guess.' "

"And what does she expect Miss Raybold and her brother to do?" asked Mrs. Archibald.

"When she had finished she got up," Clyde answered, "and went away, merely remarking that the victuals were there, and when the others were ready for them they might come and get them."

"I hope," said Mr. Archibald, "that Matlack will not fancy that sort of a hermit life. But as for me, I am greatly taken with the scheme. I think I shall like it. Is Miss Raybold about yet?"

"I see nothing of her," said Clyde, looking over towards her tent.

"Good," said Mr. Archibald, rising. "Harriet, if you want me, I shall be in my cave."

"And where is that?" she asked.

"Oh, I can't say exactly where it will be," he answered, "but if you will go down to the shore of the lake and blow four times on the dinner-horn I'll come to you, cave and all. I can easily pull it over the water."

"You forget," said Mrs. Archibald, with a smile, "that we are associate hermits."

"No, I do not," said her husband, "I remember it, and that is the reason I am off before Miss Raybold emerges upon the scene."

"I do not know," said Mrs. Archibald to Clyde, "exactly how I am going to assert myself to-day, but I shall do it one way or the other ; I am not going to be left out in the cold."

Clyde smiled, but he had no suggestion to offer ; his mind was filled with the conjecture as to what sort of a hermit life Margery was going to lead, and if she had already begun it. But just then the bishop came up, and together they went to carry the tent back to Camp Roy.

It was at least an hour afterwards, and Mrs. Archibald was comfortably seated in the shade darning stockings, with an open book in her lap. Sometimes she would read a little in the book, and then she would make some long and careful stitches in the stocking, and then she would look about her as if she greatly enjoyed combining her work and her recreation in such a lovely place on such a lovely summer morning. During one of these periods of observation she perceived Corona Raybold approaching.

"Good-morning," said the elder lady. "Is this your first appearance?"

"Yes," said Corona, with a gentle smile. "When I woke this morning I found myself to be an individual who liked to lie in bed and gaze out through an open fold in my tent upon the world beyond, and so I lay and dozed and gazed, until I felt like getting up, and then I got up, and you cannot imagine how bright and happy I felt as I thought of what I had been doing. For one morning at least I had been true to myself, without regard to other people or what they might think about it. To-morrow, if I feel like it, I shall rise at dawn, and go out and look at the stars struggling with Aurora. Whatever my personal instincts happen to be, I shall be loyal to them. Now how do you propose to assert your individuality?"

"Unfortunately," said Mrs. Archibald, "I cannot do that exactly as I would like to. If we had not promised my daughter and her husband that we would stay away for a month, I should go directly home and superintend my jelly-making and fruit-preserving ; but as I cannot do that, I have determined to act out my own self here. I shall darn stockings and sew or read, and try to make myself comfortable and happy, just as I would if I were sitting on my broad piazza at home."

"Good !" said Corona. "I think it likely that you will be more true to yourself than any of us. Doubtless you were born to be the head of a domestic household, and if you followed your own inclination you would be that if you were adrift with your family on a raft in the middle of the ocean. Now I am going away to see what further suggestions my nature has to offer me. What is Mr. Archibald doing ?"

Mrs. Archibald smiled. She knew what Corona's nature would suggest if she met a man who could talk, or rather, listen. "Oh, his nature has prompted him to hie away to the haunts of game, and to stay there until he is half starved."

Miss Raybold heaved a little sigh. " I see very few persons about here," she said—"only the two guides, in fact."

"Yes," said Mrs. Archibald, "the bishop has gone to help Mr. Clyde with his tent."

Corona moved slowly away, and as she walked her nature suggested that she would better eat something, so she repaired to the scene of Mrs. Perkenpine's ordinary operations. There she found that good woman stretched flat on her back on the ground, fast asleep. Her face and

M   177

body were shaded by some overhanging branches, but her great feet were illumined and gilded by the blazing sun. On a camp table near by were the remains of the breakfast. It had been there for two or three hours. Arthur Raybold had taken what he wanted and had gone, and before composing herself for her nap Mrs. Perkenpine had thrown over it a piece of mosquito-netting.

Corona smiled. "Their natures are coming out beautifully," she said. "It really does me good to see how admirably the scheme is unfolding itself." She sat down and ate what she could find to her taste, but it was not much. "I shall send for some fruit and some biscuit and some other little things," she thought, "that I can keep in my tent and eat when I please. That will suit me much better than the ordinary meals." Then, without awakening Mrs. Perkenpine, she strolled away, directing her steps towards Camp Roy.

When Margery had gone to her room, and had changed her wet clothes, she was thoroughly miserable. For some time she sat on the side of her little cot, unwilling to go out, on account of a nervous fear that she might meet Mr. Raybold. Of course, if he should again speak to her as he had done, she would immediately appeal to Mr. Archibald, but she did not want to do this, for she had a very strong desire not to make any trouble or divisions in the camp; so she lay down to think over the matter, and in less than two minutes she was asleep. Mrs. Archibald had come to call her to breakfast, but upon being told that she had been up ever so long, and had had her breakfast, she left the girl to her nap.

"I shall sleep here," thought Margery, "until they have all gone to do whatever it is they want to do, and then perhaps I may have a little peace."

When she awoke it was nearly eleven o'clock, and she went immediately to her little side window, from which she could see the lake and a good deal of the camp-ground. The first thing which met her reconnoitring gaze was a small boat some distance out on the lake. Its oars were revolving slowly, something like a pair of wheels with one paddle each, and it was occupied by one person. This person was Arthur Raybold, who had found the bishop calking the boat, and as soon as this work was finished, had moodily declared that he would take a row in her. He had not yet had a chance to row a boat which was in a decent condition. He wanted to be alone with his aspirations. He thought it would be scarcely wise to attempt to speak to Margery again that morning; he would give her time for her anger to cool. She was only a woman, and he knew women!

"It's that Raybold," said Margery. "He knows no more about rowing than a cat, and he's floating sideways down the lake. Good! Now I can go out and hope to be let alone. I don't know when he will ever get that boat back again. Perhaps never."

She was not a wicked girl, and she did not desire that the awkward rower might never get back; but still she did not have that dread of an accident which might have come over her had the occupant of the boat been a brother or any one she cared very much about. She took a novel, of which, during her whole stay in camp, she had read perhaps ten pages, and left the cabin, this time by the door.

"How does your individuality treat you?" asked Mrs. Archibald, as Margery approached her.

"Oh, horribly, so far," was the answer; "but I think it is going to do better. I shall find some nice place where I can read and be undisturbed. I can think of nothing pleasanter such a morning as this."

"I am very much mistaken in your nature," thought Mrs. Archibald, "if that is the sort of thing that suits you."

"Martin," said Margery, not in the least surprised that she should meet the young guide within the next three minutes, "do you know of some really nice secluded spot where I can sit and read, and not be bothered? I don't mean that place where you hung the hammock. I don't want to go there again."

Martin was pale, and his voice trembled as he spoke. "Miss Dearborn," said he, "I think it is a wicked and a burning shame that you should be forced to look for a hiding-place where you may hope to rest undisturbed if that scoundrel in the boat out there should happen to fancy to come ashore. But you needn't do it. There is no necessity for it. Go where you please, sit where you please, and do what you please, and I will see to it that you are not disturbed."

"Oh, no, no!" exclaimed Margery. "That would never do. I know very well that you could keep him away from me, and I am quite sure that you would be glad to do it, but there mustn't be anything of that kind. He is Miss Raybold's brother and—and in a way one of our camping party, and I don't want any disturbances or quarrels."

Martin's breast heaved, and he breathed heavily. "I have no doubt you are right," he said— "of course you are. But I can tell you this : if I see that fellow troubling you again I'll kill him, or—"

"Martin! Martin!" exclaimed Margery. "What do you mean? What makes you talk in this way?"

"What makes me?" he exclaimed, as if it were impossible to restrain his words. "My heart makes me, my soul makes me. I—"

"Your heart? Your soul?" interrupted Margery. "I don't understand."

For a moment he looked at the astonished girl in silence, and then he said : "Miss Dearborn, it's of no use for me to try to hide what I feel. If I hadn't got so angry I might have been able to keep quiet, but I can't do it now. If that man thinks he loves you, his love is like a grain of sand compared to mine."

"Yours?" cried Margery.

"Yes," said Martin, his face pallid and his eyes sparkling, "mine. You may think it is an insult for me to talk this way, but love is love, and it will spring up where it pleases ; and besides, I am not the common sort of a fellow you may think I am. After saying what I have said, I am bound to say more. I belong to a good family, and am college bred. I am poor, and I love nature. I am working to make money to travel and become a naturalist. I prefer this sort of work because it takes me into the heart of nature. I am not ashamed of what I am, I am not ashamed of my work, and my object in life is a nobler one, I think, than the practice of the law, or a great many other things like it."

Margery stood and looked at him with wide-open eyes. "Do you mean to say," she said, "that you want to marry me? It would take years and years for you to become naturalist enough to support a wife."

"I have made no plans," he said, quickly, "I have no purpose. I did not intend to tell you now that I love you, but since I have said that, I will say also that with you to fight for there could be no doubt about my success. I should be bound to succeed. It would be impossible for me to fail. As for the years, I would wait, no matter how many they should be."

He spoke with such hot earnestness that Margery involuntarily drew herself a little away from him. At this the flush went out of his face.

"Oh, Miss Dearborn," he exclaimed, "don't think that I am like that man out there! Don't think that I will persecute you if you don't wish to hear me; that I will follow you about and make your life miserable. If you say to me that you do not wish to see me again, you will never see me again. Say what you please, and you will find that I am a gentleman."

She could see that now. She felt sure that if she told him she did not wish ever to see him again he would never appear before her. But what would he do? She was not in the least afraid of him, but his fierce earnestness frightened her, not for herself, but for him. Suddenly a thought struck her.

"Martin," said she, "I don't doubt in the least that what you have said to me about yourself is true. You are as good as other people, although you do happen now to be a guide, and perhaps after a while you may be very well off; but for all that you are a guide, and you are in Mr. Sadler's employment, and Mr. Sadler's rights and powers are just like gas escaping from a pipe : they are everywhere from cellar to garret, so to speak, and you couldn't escape them. It would be a bad, bad thing for you, Martin, if he were to hear that you make propositions of the kind you have made to the ladies that he pays you to take out into the woods to guide and to protect."

Martin was on the point of a violent expostulation, but she stopped him.

"Now I know what you are going to say," she exclaimed, "but it isn't of any use. You are in his employment, and you are bound to honor and to respect him ; that is the way a guide can show himself to be a gentleman."

"But suppose," said Martin, quickly, "that he, knowing my family as he does, should think I had done wisely in speaking to you."

A cloud came over her brow. It annoyed her that he should thus parry her thrust.

"Well, you can ask him," she said, abruptly ;

"and if he doesn't object, you can go to see my mother, when she gets home, and ask her. And here comes Mr. Matlack. I think he has been calling you. Now don't say another word, unless it is about fish."

But Matlack did not come; he stopped and called, and Martin went to him.

Margery walked languidly towards the woods and sat down on the projecting root of a large tree. Then leaning back against the trunk, she sighed.

"It is a perfectly dreadful thing to be a girl," she said; "but I am glad I did not speak to him as I did to Mr. Raybold. I believe he would have jumped into the lake."

CHAPTER XXI

"MARTIN," said Matlack, sharply, before the young man had reached him, "it seems to me that you think that you have been engaged here as lady's-maid, but there's other things to do besides teaching young women about trees and fishes. If you think," continued Matlack, when the two had reached the woodland kitchen, "that your bein' a hermit is goin' to let you throw all the work on me, you're mistaken. There's a lot of potatoes that's got to be peeled for dinner."

Without a word Martin sat down on the ground with a pan of potatoes in front of him and began to work. Had he been a proud crusader setting forth to fight the Saracens his blood could not have coursed with greater warmth and force, his soul could not have more truly spurned the earth and all the common things upon it. What he had said to Margery had made him feel ennobled. If Raybold had that instant appeared before him with some jeering insult, Martin would have pardoned him with lofty scorn; and yet he peeled potatoes, and did it well. But his thoughts were not upon his work ; they were upon the future which, if he proved himself to be the man he thought himself to be, might open before him.

When he had finished the potatoes he put the pan upon a table and stood near by, deep in thought.

"Yes," said he to himself, "I should go now. After what I have said to her I cannot stay here and live this life before her. I would wait on her with bended knee at every step, but with love for her in my soul I cannot wash dishes for other people. I have spoken, and now I must act ; and the quicker the better. If all goes well I may be here again, but I shall not come back as a guide." Then a thought of Raybold crossed his mind, but he put it aside. Even if he stayed here he could not protect her, for she had shown that she did not wish him to do it in the only way he could do it, and he felt sure, too, that any further annoyance would result in an appeal to Mr. Archibald.

"Well," said Matlack, sharply, "what's the matter with you ? Don't you intend to move ?"

"Yes," said Martin, turning quickly, "I do intend to move. I am going to leave this camp just as soon as I can pack my things."

" And where in the name of thunder are you goin' to ?"

"I'm going to Sadler's," said Martin.

"What for ?"

"On my own business," was the reply.

Matlack looked at him for a moment suspiciously. "Have you got any complaints to make of me ?" he said.

"No," said Martin, promptly, "not one; but I have affairs on hand which will take me off immediately."

"Before dinner ?" asked Matlack.

"Yes," said the other, "before dinner; now."

"Go ahead then," said Matlack, putting some sticks of wood into the stove; "and tell Sadler that if he don't send me somebody before supper-time to help about this camp, he'll see me. I'll be hanged," he said to himself, as he closed the door of the stove, "if this isn't hermitism with a vengeance. I wonder who'll be the next one to cut and run; most likely it will be Mrs. Perkenpine."

Early in the afternoon, warm and dusty, Martin presented himself before Peter Sadler, who was smoking his pipe on the little shaded piazza at the back of the house.

"Oh, ho!" said Peter. "How in the name of common-sense did you happen to turn up at this minute? This is about as queer a thing as I've known of lately. What did you come for? Sit down."

"Mr. Sadler," said Martin, "I have come here on most important business."

"Lake dry?" asked Peter.

"It is a matter," said Martin, "which concerns myself; and if all the lakes in the world were dry, I would not be able to think about them, so full is my soul of one thing."

"By the Lord Harry," said Peter, "let's have it, quick!"

In a straightforward manner, but with an ardent vehemence which he could not repress, Martin stated his business with Peter Sadler. He told him how he loved Margery, what he had said to her, and what she had said to him.

"And now," said the young man, "I have

come to ask your permission to address her; but whether you give it or not I shall go to her mother and speak to her. I know her address, and I intend to do everything in an honorable way."

Peter Sadler put down his pipe and looked steadfastly at the young man. "I wish to Heaven," said he, "that there was a war goin' on! I'd write a letter to the commander-in-chief and let you take it to him, and I'd tell him you was the bravest man between Hudson Bay and Patagonia. By George! I can't understand it! I can't understand how you could have the cheek, the unutterable brass, to come here and ask me— me, Peter Sadler — to let you court one of the ladies in a campin'-party of mine. And, what's more, I can't understand how I can sit here and hear you tell me that tale without picking up a chair and knocking you down with it."

"Mr. Sadler," said Martin, rising, "I have spoken to you fairly and squarely, and if that's all you've got to say, I will go."

"Sit down!" roared Peter, bringing his hand upon the table as if he would drive it's legs through the floor. "Sit down, and listen to what I have to say to you. It's the strangest thing that ever happened to me that I am not more angry with you than I am; but I can't understand it, and I pass it by. Now that you are seated again, I will make some remarks on my side. Do you see that?" said he, picking up a letter on the table. "Do you see who it is addressed to?"

"To me!" exclaimed Martin, in surprise.

188

"Yes, it's to you," said Peter, "and I wrote it,
and I intended to send it by Bill Hammond this
afternoon. That's the reason I was surprised
when I saw you here. But I'm not goin' to give
it to you; I'd rather tell you what's in it, now
you are here. Before I knew you were the abject
ninnyhammer that you have just told me you
are I had a good opinion of you, and thought that
you were cut out to make a first-class traveller
and explorer — the sort of a fellow who could
lead a surveying expedition through the wilderness, or work up new countries and find out what
they are made of and what's in them. Only yesterday I heard of a chance that ought to make
you jump, and this morning I wrote to you about
it. A friend of mine, who's roughed it with me
for many a day, is goin' to take an expedition
down into New Mexico in the interests of a railroad and minin' company. They want to know
everything about the country — the game, fish,
trees, and plants, as well as the minerals—and it
struck me that if you are not just the kind of
man they want you could make yourself so in
a very short time. They'd pay you well enough,
and you'd have a chance to dip into natural history, and all that sort of thing, that you had no
reason to expect for a dozen years to come, if it
ever came. If such a chance had been offered
to me at your age I wouldn't have changed lots
with a king. All you've got to do is to pack
up and be off. The party starts from New York
in just three days; I'll give you a letter to
Joe Hendricks, and that 'll be all you want. He
knows me well enough to take you without a
189

word. If you haven't got money enough saved
to fit yourself out for the trip I'll lend you some,
and you can pay me back when they pay you.
You can take the train this afternoon and maybe
you can see Hendricks to-night. So pack up
what you want and leave what you don't want,
and I'll take care of it. I'll write to Hendricks
now."

Many times did the face of Martin flush and
pale as he listened. A vision of Paradise had
been opened before him, but he felt that he must
shut his eyes.

" Mr. Sadler," he said, " you are very kind. You
offer me a great thing—a thing which two weeks
ago I should have accepted in the twinkling of an
eye, and would have thanked you for all the rest
of my life ; but I cannot take it now. With all
my heart I love a woman ; I have told her so,
and I am now going on the path she told me to
take. I cannot turn aside from that for any prospects in the world."

Peter Sadler's face grew red, and then it grew
black, and then it turned red again, and finally
resumed its ordinary brown.

"Martin Sanders," said he, speaking quietly,
but with one hand fastened upon the arm of his
chair with a grasp which a horse could not have
loosened, " if you are cowardly enough and small
enough and paltry enough to go to a girl who is
living in peace and comfort and ask her to marry
you, when you know perfectly well that for years
to come you could not give her a decent roof over
her head, and that if her family wanted her to
live like a Christian they would have to give her

the money to do it with ; and if you are fool
enough not to know that when she sent you first
to me and then to her mother she was tryin' to
get rid of you without hurtin' your feelin's, why,
then, I want you to get out of my sight, and the
quicker the better. But if you are not so low
down as that, go to your room and pack up your
bag. The coach will start for the train at three
o'clock, and it is now nearly half-past two ; that
will just give me time to write to Hendricks.
Go !"

Martin rose. Whatever happened afterwards,
he must go now. It seemed to him as if the
whole world had suddenly grown colder ; as if
he had been floating in a fog and had neared an
iceberg. Could it be possible that she had spoken,
as she had spoken, simply to get rid of him ? He
could not believe it. No one with such honest
eyes could speak in that way ; and yet he did not
know what to believe.

In any case, he would go away in the coach.
He had spoken to Sadler, and now, whether he
spoke to any one else or not, the sooner he left
the better.

When he came to take the coach, Peter Sadler,
who had rolled himself to the front of the house,
handed him the letter he had written.

" I believe you are made of the right kind of
stuff," he said, " although you've got a little
mouldy by bein' lazy out there in the woods,
but you're all right now ; and what you've got
to do is to go ahead with a will, and, take my
word for it, you'll come out on top. Do you
want any money ? No ? Very well, then, good-

bye. You needn't trouble yourself to write to me, I'll hear about you from Hendricks; and I'd rather know what he thinks about you than what you think about yourself."

"How little you know," thought Martin, as he entered the coach, "what I am or what I think about myself. As if my purpose could be changed by words of yours!" And he smiled a smile which would have done justice to Arthur Raybold. The chill had gone out of him; he was warm again.

On the train he read the letter to Hendricks which Peter Sadler had given to him unsealed. It was a long letter, and he read it twice. Then he sat and gazed out of the window at the flying scenery for nearly half an hour, after which he read the letter again. Then he folded it up and put it into his pocket.

"If she had given me the slightest reason to hope," he said to himself, "how easy it would be to tear this letter into scraps."

Now an idea came into his mind. If he could see her mother quickly, and if she should ignore his honorable intentions and refuse to give him the opportunity to prove that he was worthy of a thought from her and her daughter, then it might not be too late to fall back on Peter Sadler's letter. But he shook his head; that would be dishonorable and unworthy of him.

He shut his eyes; he could not bear to look at the brightness of the world outside the window of the car. Under his closed lids there came to him visions, sometimes of Margery and sometimes of the forests of New Mexico. Sometimes

the visions were wavering, uncertain, and tran-
sitory, and again they were strong and vivid—
so plain to him that he could almost hear the
leaves rustle as some wild creature turned a
startled look upon him.

That night he delivered his letter to Mr. Hendricks.

CHAPTER XXII

AFTER Martin had left her, Margery sat on the root of the tree until Mr. Clyde came up and said he had been wondering what had become of her.

"I have been wondering that, myself," she said. "At least, I have been wondering what is going to become of me."

"Don't you intend to be a hermit?" said he.

She shook her head. "I don't think it is possible," she answered. "There is no one who is better satisfied to be alone, and who can make herself happier all by herself, and who, in all sorts of ways, can get along better without other people than I can, and yet other people are continually interfering with me, and I cannot get away from them."

Clyde smiled. "That is a pretty plain hint," he said. "I suppose I might as well take it, and go off to some hermitage of my own."

"Oh, nonsense!" said Margery. "Don't be so awfully quick in coming to conclusions. I do feel worried and troubled and bothered, and I want some one to talk to; not about things which worry me, of course, but about common, ordinary things, that will make me forget."

A slight shade came over the face of Mr. Clyde,

194

and he seated himself on the ground near Margery. "It is a shame," said he, "that you should be worried. What is it in this peaceable, beautiful forest troubles you?"

"Did you ever hear of a paradise without snakes?" she asked. "The very beauty of it makes them come here."

"I have never yet known any paradise at all," he replied. "But can't you tell me what it is that troubles you?"

Margery looked at him with her clear, large eyes. "I'll tell you," she said, "if you will promise not to do a single thing without my permission."

"I promise that," said Clyde, eagerly.

"I am troubled by people making love to me."

"People!" exclaimed Clyde, with a puzzled air.

"Yes," said she. "Your cousin is one of them."

"I might have supposed that; but who on earth can be the other one?"

"That is Martin," said Margery.

For a moment Mr. Clyde did not seem to understand, and then he exclaimed: "You don't mean the young man who cuts wood and helps Matlack?"

"Yes, I do," she answered. "And you need not shut your jaw hard and grit your teeth that way. That is exactly what he did when he found out about Mr. Raybold. It is of no use to get angry, for you can't do anything without my permission; and, besides, I tell you that if I were condemned by a court to be made love to, I would much rather have Martin make it than Mr. Raybold. Martin is a good deal more than a guide; he has a good education, and would not be here if it were not for his love of nature. He is going to make nature his object in life, and there is something noble in that; a great deal better than trying to strut about on the stage."

"And those two have really been making love to you?" asked Clyde.

"Yes, really," she answered. "You never saw people more in earnest in all your life. As for Mr. Raybold, he was as earnest as a cat after a bird. He made me furiously angry. Martin was different. He is just as earnest, but he is more of a gentleman; and when I told him what I wanted him to do, he said he would do it. But there is no use in telling your cousin what I want him to do. He is determined to persecute me and make me miserable, and there is no way of stopping it, except by making a quarrel between him and Uncle Archibald. It is a shame!" she went on. "Who could have thought that two people would have turned up to disturb me in this way."

"Margery," said Mr. Clyde, and although he called her by her Christian name she took no notice of it, "you think you have too many lovers: but you are mistaken. You have not enough; you ought to have three."

She looked at him inquiringly.

"Yes," he said, quickly, "and I want to be the third."

"And so make matters three times as bad as they were at first?" she asked.

"Not at all," said he. "When you have chosen one of them, he could easily keep away the two others."

" Do you mean," said Margery, " that if I were to agree to have three, and then, if I were to ask you to do it, you would go away quietly with one of the others and leave me in peace with the third one?"

Mr. Clyde half smiled, but instantly grew serious again, and a flush came on his face. " Margery," said he, " I cannot bear trifling any more about this. No matter what anybody has said to you, whether it is any one in this camp or any one out of it, there is not a man in this world who—"

" Oh, Mr. Clyde," interrupted Margery, " you must not sit there and speak to me in such an excited way. If any one should see us they would think we were quarrelling. Let us go down to the lake ; the air from the water is cool and soothing."

Together they walked from under the shade of the tree, and so wended their way that it brought them to a mass of shrubbery which edged the water a little distance down the lake. On the other side of this shrubbery was a pretty bank, which they had seen before.

" It always tranquillizes me," said Margery, as they stood side by side on the bank, " to look out over the water. Doesn't it have that effect on you?"

" No !" exclaimed Clyde. " It does not tranquillize me a bit. Nothing could tranquillize me at a moment like this. Margery, I want you to know that I love you. I did not intend to tell you so soon, but what you have said makes it necessary. I have loved you ever since I met you at Peter Sadler's, and, no matter what you say about it, I shall love you to the end of my life."

"Even if I should send you away with one of the others?"

"Yes; no matter what you did."

"That would be wrong," she said.

"It doesn't matter. Right or wrong, I'd do it."

Margery gave him a glance from which it would have been impossible to eliminate all signs of admiration. "And if I were to arrange it otherwise," she said, "would you undertake to keep the others away?"

There was no answer to this question, but in a minute afterwards Clyde exclaimed: "Do you think any one would dare to come near you if they saw you now?"

"Hardly," said Margery, raising her head from his shoulder and looking up into his sparkling eyes. "Really, Harrison, you ought not to speak in such a loud voice. If Aunt Harriet were to hear you she might dare to come."

Margery was late to dinner, although the horn was blown three times.

Much to the surprise of his wife, Mr. Archibald returned to camp about an hour before dinner.

"How is this?" she exclaimed. "Wasn't the fishing good?"

"I have had a disagreeable experience," he said, "and I will tell you about it. I was fishing in a little cove some distance down the lake and having good sport, when I heard a thumping, and looking around I saw Raybold in a boat rowing

towards me. I suppose he thought he was rowing, but he was really floating with the current;
but as he neared me he suddenly pulled his boat
towards me with such recklessness that I was
afraid he would run into me. I considered his
rowing into the cove to be a piece of bad manners, for of course it would spoil my fishing, but
I had no idea he actually intended to lay along-
side of me. This he did, however, and so awkwardly that his boat struck mine with such force
that it half tipped it over. Then he lay hold of
my gunwale, and said he had something to say
to me.

"I was as angry as if a man in the street had
knocked my hat down over my eyes and said that
he did so in order to call my attention to a sub-
scription paper. But this indignation was nothing to what I felt when the fellow began to
speak. I cannot repeat his words, but he stated
his object at once, and said that as this was a
good opportunity to speak to me alone, he wished
to ask me to remove what he called the utterly
useless embargo which I had placed upon him in
regard to Margery. He said it was useless because he could not be expected to give up his
hopes and his plans simply because I objected to
them; and he went on to say that if I understood him fully, and if Margery understood him,
he did not believe that either of us would object.
And then he actually asked me to use my influ-
ence with her to make her listen to him. From
what he said, I am sure he has been speaking to
her. I did not let him finish, but turned and
blazed at him in words as strong as would come

to me. I ordered him never to speak to me again or show himself in my camp, and told him that if he did either of these things he would do them at his peril; and then, for fear he might say something which would make me lose control of myself, I jerked up my anchor and rowed away from him. I didn't feel like fishing any more, and so I came back."

"His behavior is shameful," said Mrs. Archibald. "And what is more, it is ridiculous, for Margery would not look at him. What sort of a man does he think you are, to suppose that you would give your permission to any one, no matter who he might be, to offer marriage to a young lady in your charge? But what are you going to do about it? I think it very likely he will come to this camp, and he may speak to you."

"In that case I shall have him driven out," said Mr. Archibald, "as if he were a drunken vagabond. Personally I shall have nothing to do with him, but I shall order my guides to eject him."

"I hope that may not be necessary," said his wife. "It would make bad feeling, and deeply wound his sister, for it would be the same thing as putting her out. She talks too much, to be sure, but she is a lady, and has treated us all very courteously. I wish we could get through the rest of our stay here without any disturbance or bad feeling."

"I wish so too, with all my heart," said her husband. "And the only thing necessary to that end is that that ass Raybold shall keep out of my sight."

It was about two o'clock that afternoon, and Mrs. Archibald, under her tree, her basket of stockings all darned and her novel at its culminating point of interest, was the only visible occupant of Camp Rob, when Corona Raybold came walking towards her, an obvious purpose in her handsome face, which was somewhat flushed by exercise.

"I do not think," she said, as soon as she was near enough for Mrs. Archibald to hear her, "that the true purpose and intention of our plan is properly understood by all of the party. I think, after some explanation, everything will go well, but I have been endeavoring for the last half-hour to find Mrs. Perkenpine, and have utterly failed. I am very hungry, but I can discover nothing to eat. All our stores appear to be absolutely raw, or in some intermediate state of crudity. I intend to order some provisions in cans or boxes which will be at all times available, but I have not done so yet, and so I have come over to speak to you about the matter. Did your guides prepare your dinner as usual?"

"Oh yes," said Mrs. Archibald. "A hermit life seems to make no difference with Mr. Matlack. We become associates at meal-times, but, as you see, we have separated again."

"I must instil into Mrs. Perkenpine's mind," said Corona, "that, in order thoroughly to act out her own nature, she must cook and do other things of a domestic character. Of course she will do those things in her own way; that is to be expected; but she must do them. It is impossible to imagine a woman of her class whose soul is not set more or less upon domestic affairs. I will instance Mr. Matlack. His nature belongs to the woods and the out-of-door world, and that nature prompts him to cook what he shoots."

Mrs. Archibald laughed. "I think his nature is a very good one," she said, "and I will go with you to find him and see if he cannot give you a luncheon, if not a dinner."

"Thank you very much," said Corona; "but indeed I do not wish to trouble you. I will go to him myself. You are very kind, but it is not in the least degree necessary for you to accompany me. A cup of tea and some little trifle is all I shall ask him for."

For a moment Mrs. Archibald hesitated, and then she said, "As we are hermits, I suppose we must not keep together any more than we can help, and so I will let you go alone."

Corona found Phil Matlack by his kitchen tent, busily engaged in rubbing the inside of a large kettle. He was not in a good humor. The departure of Martin had thrown all the work of his camp upon him, and now the appearance of a person from another camp requesting to be fed aroused him to absolute anger. He did not scold, for it would have been impossible to look at that beautiful and imperturbable face and say hard words to it. He did not refuse the cup of tea or the bread-and-butter for which he was asked, and he even added some cold meat; but he indignantly made up his mind that he would stand no more of this nonsense, and that if necessary he would go to Sadler and throw up the job. He had not engaged to cook for three camps.

" HAVEN'T TRIED IT "

Miss Raybold did not appear to notice his state of mind, and ate heartily. She thought it was fortunate that he happened to have the kettle on the stove, and she asked him how he liked the hermit life—the living for himself alone.

" Haven't tried it," he answered, curtly.

" I understand," said Corona, " you have had to live too much for other people ; but it is too soon to expect our plan to run smoothly. In a short time, however, we shall be better able to know our own natures and show them to others."

" Oh, I can do that," said he ; " and I am goin' to, precious soon."

" I have no doubt of it," she answered. " And now can you tell me where Mr. Archibald has gone ? I did not see him this morning, and there are some matters I wish to speak to him about."

" No, miss," said Matlack, promptly, " I don't know where he is. He's a real hermit. He's off by himself, most likely miles away."

Corona reflected. " Mr.—the bishop ? Have you seen him ? He may be able to—"

The guide grinned grimly. He had seen the man of muscle—not fat—conversing that morning with Corona, and an hour afterwards he had seen him, not in the same place, but in the same companionship, and it gave him a certain pleasure to know that the man who could heave rocks and break young trees could not relieve himself from the thralls of the lady of the flowing speech.

" The bishop ?" said he. " Don't you know where he went to ?"

" He left me," she answered, " because he was

obliged to go to prepare dinner for my brother and Mr. Clyde ; but he is not in Camp Roy now, for I went there to look for Mrs. Perkenpine."

"Well," said the wicked Matlack, pointing to the spot where, not long before, Margery had found a tranquillizing breeze, "I saw him going along with a book a little while ago, and I think he went down to the shore, just beyond that clump of bushes over there. He seems to be a man who likes readin', which isn't a bad thing for a hermit."

"Thank you," said Miss Raybold, rising. "I do not care for anything more. You are very kind, and I am quite sure I shall not have to trouble you again. To-morrow everything will be running smoothly."

Matlack looked at her as she quietly walked away. "She's a pretty sort of a hermit," he said to himself. "If she really had to live by herself she'd cut out a wooden man and talk to it all day. It won't be long before she accidentally stumbles over that big fellow with his book."

CHAPTER XXIII

THE mind of the guide was comforted and re-
lieved that he had got the better of the bishop in
one way, although he could not do it in another.
But he did not relinquish his purpose of putting
an end to the nonsense which made him do the
work of other people, and as soon as he had set
his kitchen in order he started out to find Mrs.
Perkenpine. A certain amount of nonsense from
the people in camp might have to be endured,
but nonsense from Mrs. Perkenpine was something about which Peter Sadler would have a
word to say.

Matlack was a good hunter. He could follow
all sorts of tracks — rabbit tracks, bird tracks,
deer tracks, and the tracks of big ungainly shoes
—and in less than half an hour he had reached a
cluster of moss-covered rocks lying some distance
back in the woods, and approached by the bed of
a now dry stream. Sitting on one of these rocks,
her back against a tree, her straw hat lying beside her, and her dishevelled hair hanging about
her shoulders, was Mrs. Perkenpine, reading a
newspaper. At the sound of his footsteps she
looked up.

"Well, I'll be bound !" she said. "If I'd crawl into a fox-hole I expect you'd come and sniff in after me."

Matlack stood and looked at her for a moment. He could not help smiling at the uncomfortable manner in which she was trying to make herself comfortable on those rough rocks.

"I'll tell you what it is, Mrs. Perkenpine," he said, "you'll get yourself into the worst kind of a hole if you go off this way, leavin' everything at sixes and sevens behind you."

"It's my nater," said she. "I'm findin' it out and gittin' it ready to show to other people. You're the fust one that's seed it. How do you like it ?"

"I don't like it at all," said the guide, "and I have just come to tell you that if you don't go back to your tent and cook supper to-night and attend to your business, I'll walk over to Sadler's, and tell Peter to send some one in your place. I'm goin' over there anyway, if he don't send a man to take Martin's place."

"Peter Sadler !" ejaculated Mrs. Perkenpine, letting her tumbled newspaper fall into her lap. "He's a man that knows his own nater, and lets other people see it. He lives his own life, if anybody does. He's individdle down to the heels, and just look at him ! He's the same as a king. I tell you, Phil Matlack, that the more I knows myself, just me, the more I'm tickled. It seems like scootin' round in the woods, findin' all sorts of funny hoppin' things and flowers that you never seed before. Why, it 'ain't been a whole day since I begun knowin' myself, and I've found out lots. I used to think that I liked to cook and clean up, but I don't; I hate it."

Matlack smiled, and taking out his pipe, he lighted it and sat down on a rock.

"I do believe," he said, "that you are the most out and out hermit of the whole lot; but it won't do, and if you don't get over your objections to cookin' you'll have to walk out of these woods to-morrow."

Mrs. Perkenpine sat and looked at her companion a few moments without giving any apparent heed to his remarks.

"Of course," said she, "it isn't only findin' out what you be yourself, but it's lettin' other people see what you be. If you didn't do that it would be like a pot a-b'ilin' out in the middle of a prairie, with nobody nearer nor a hundred miles."

"It would be the same as if it hadn't b'iled," remarked Matlack.

"That's jest it," said she, "and so I ain't sorry you come along, Phil, so's I can tell you some things I've found out about myself. One of them is that I like to lie flat on my back and look up at the leaves of the trees and think about them."

"What do you think?" asked Matlack.

"I don't think nothin'," said she. "Just as soon as I begin to look at them wrigglin' in the wind, and I am beginnin' to wonder what it is I think about them, I go slam bang to sleep, and when I wake up and try to think again what it is I think, off I go again. But I like it. If I don't know what it is I think, I ought to know that I don't know it. That's what I call bein' really and truly a hermick."

"What else did you find out?" inquired Matlack.

"I found out," she answered, with animation, "that I admire to read anecdotes. I didn't know I cared a pin for anecdotes until I took to hermickin'. Now here's this paper; it came 'round the cheese, and it's got a good many anecdotes scattered about in it. Let me read one of them to you. It's about a man who made his will and afterwards was a-drivin' a horse along a road, and the horse got skeered and ran over his executor, who was takin' a walk. Then he sung out, 'Oh, bless my soul!' says he. But I'll read you the rest if I can find it."

"Never mind about the anecdote," said Matlack, who knew very well that it would take Mrs. Perkenpine half an hour to spell out twenty lines in a newspaper. "What I want to know is if you found out anything about yourself that's likely to give you a boost in the direction of that cookin'-stove of yourn."

Mrs. Perkenpine was a woman whose remarks did not depend upon the remarks of others. "Phil Matlack," said she, gazing fixedly at his pipe, "if I had a man I'd let him smoke just as much as he pleased and just where he pleased. He could smoke afore he got up, and he could smoke at his meals, and he could smoke after he went to bed, and, if he fancied that sort of thing, he could smoke at family prayers; it wouldn't make no difference to me, and I wouldn't say a word to him agin' it. If that was his individdlety, I'd say viddle."

"And how about everything else?" asked Mat-

lack. "Would you tell him to cook his own victuals and mend his clothes accordin' to his own
nater ?"

"No, sir," said she, striking with her expansive
hand the newspaper in her lap—"no, sir. I'd get
up early in the mornin', and cook and wash and
bake and scour. I'd skin the things he shot, and
clean his fish, and dig bait if he wanted it. I'd
tramp into the woods after him, and carry the
gun and the victuals and fishin'-poles, and I'd set
traps and row a boat and build fires, and let him
go along and work out his own nater smokin' or
in any other way he was born to. That's the biggest thing I've found out about myself. I never
knowed, until I began, this mornin', explorin' of
my own nater, what a powerful hard thing it is,
when I'm thinkin' of my own individdlety, to keep
somebody else's individdlety from poppin' up in
front of it, and so says I to myself, 'If I can think
of both them individdleties at the same time it
will suit me fust-rate.' And when you come
along I thought I'd let you know what sort of a
nater I've got, for it ain't likely you'd ever find it
out for yourself. And now that we're in that
business—"

"Hello !" cried Matlack, springing to his feet.
"There is somebody callin' me. Who's there ?"
he shouted, stepping out into the bed of the
stream.

A call was now heard, and in a few moments
the bishop appeared some distance below.

"Mr. Matlack," he said, "there's a man at your
camp inquiring for you. He came from Sadler's,
and I've been looking high and low for you."

"A man from Sadler's," said Matlack, turning to Mrs. Perkenpine, "and I must be off to see him. Remember what I told you about the supper." And so saying, he walked rapidly away.

Out in the open Matlack found the bishop. "Obliged to you for lookin' me up," he said, "it's a pity to give you so much trouble."

"Oh, don't mention it!" exclaimed the bishop. "You cannot understand, perhaps, not knowing the circumstances, but I assure you I never was more obliged to any one than to that man who wants to see you and couldn't find you. There was no one else to look for you, and I simply had to go."

"You are not goin' to walk back to camp?" inquired Matlack.

"No," replied the bishop, "now that I am here, I think I will go up the lake and try to find a very secluded spot in the shade and take a nap."

The guide smiled as he walked away. "Don't understand!" said he. "You've got the boot on the wrong leg."

Arrived at his tent, Matlack found Bill Hammond, a young man in Sadler's service, who informed him that that burly individual had sent Martin away in the stage-coach, and had ordered him to come and take his place.

"All right," said Matlack. "I guess you're as good as he was, and so you can settle down to work. By-the-way, do you know that we are all hermits here?"

"Hermits?" said the other. "What's that?"

"Why, hermits," said Matlack, "is individ'als who get up early in the mornin' and attend to their own business just as hard as they can, without lookin' to the right or left, until it's time to go to bed."

The young man looked at him in some surprise. "There's nothing so very uncommon in that," said he.

" No," replied the guide, "perhaps there ain't. But as you might hear them talkin' about hermits here, I thought I'd tell you just what sort of things they are."

CHAPTER XXIV

WHEN a strange young man assisted Matlack at the supper-table that evening, Mr. Archibald asked what had become of Martin.

"Peter Sadler has sent him away," answered the guide. "I don't know where he sent him or what he sent him for. But he's a young man who's above this sort of business, and so I suppose he's gone off to take up something that's more elevated."

"I am sorry," said Mrs. Archibald, "for I liked him."

Mr. Archibald smiled. "This business of insisting upon our own individualities," he said, "seems to have worked very promptly in his case. I suppose he found out he was fitted for something better than a guide, and immediately went off to get that better thing."

"That's about the size of it," said Matlack.

Margery said nothing. Her heart sank. She could not help feeling that what she had said to the young man had been the cause of his sudden departure. Could he have done such a thing, she thought, as really to go and ask Mr. Sadler, and, having found he did not mind, could he have gone to see her mother? Her appetite for her supper departed, and she soon rose and strolled away, and as she strolled the thought came again to her that it was a truly dreadful thing to be a girl.

Having received no orders to the contrary, Matlack, with his new assistant, built and lighted the camp-fire. Some of the hermits took this as a matter of course, and some were a little surprised, but one by one they approached ; the evening air was beginning to be cool, and the vicinity of the fire was undoubtedly the pleasantest place in camp. Soon they were all assembled but one, and Mrs. Archibald breathed freer when she found that Arthur Raybold was not there.

"I am delighted," said Corona, as soon as she took her usual seat, which was a camp-chair, "to see you all gather about the fire. I was afraid that some of you might think that because we are hermits we must keep away from each other all the time. But we must remember that we are associate hermits, and so should come together occasionally. I was going to say something to the effect that some of us may have misunderstood the true manner and intent of the assertions of our individualities, but I do not now believe that this is necessary."

"Do you mean by all that," said Mrs. Perkenpine, "that I cooked the supper ?"

"Yes," said Miss Raybold, turning upon her guide with a pleasant smile, "that is what I referred to."

"Well," said Mrs. Perkenpine, " I was told that if I didn't cook I'd be bounced. It isn't my individdlety to cook for outsiders, but it isn't my

individdlety to be bounced, nuther, so I cooked.
Is that bein' a hermick?"

"You have it," cried Mr. Archibald, "you've
not only found out what you are, but what you
have to be. Your knowledge of yourself is perfect. And now," he continued, "isn't there somebody who can tell us a story? When we are sitting around a camp-fire, there is nothing better
than stories. Bishop, I dare say you have heard
a good many in the course of your life. Don't
you feel like giving us one?"

"I think," said Corona, "that by the aid of
stories it is possible to get a very good idea of
ourselves. For instance, if some one were to tell
a good historical story, and any one of us should
find himself or herself greatly interested in it,
then that person might discover, on subsequent
reflection, some phase of his or her intellect
which he or she might not have before noticed.
On the other hand, if it should be a love story,
and some of us could not bear to hear it, then
we might also find out something about ourselves of which we had been ignorant. But I
really think that, before making any tests of this
sort, we should continue the discussion of what
is at present the main object of our lives—self-
knowledge and self-assertion. In other words,
the emancipation of the individual. As I have
said before, and as we all know, there never was
a better opportunity offered a group of people of
mature minds to subject themselves, free of outside influences, to a thorough mental inquisition,
and then to exhibit the results of their self-exam-
inations to appreciative companions. This last

is very important. If we do not announce to others what we are, it is of scarcely any use to be anything. I mean this, of course, in a limited sense."

"Harriet," said Mr. Archibald, abruptly, "do you remember where I left my pipe? I do not like this cigar."

"On the shelf by the door of the cabin," she replied. "I saw it as I came out."

Her husband immediately rose and left the fire. Corona paused in her discourse to wait until Mr. Archibald came back; but then, as if she did not wish to lose the floor, she turned towards the bishop, who sat at a little distance from her, and addressed herself to him, with the idea of making some collateral remarks on what she had already said, in order to fill up the time until Mr. Archibald should return.

Mrs. Archibald thought that her husband had been a little uncivil; but almost immediately after he had gone, she, too, jumped up, and, without making any excuse whatever, hurried after him

The reason for this sudden movement was that Mrs. Archibald had seen some one approaching from the direction of Camp Roy. She instantly recognized this person as Arthur Raybold, and felt sure that, unwilling to stay longer by himself, he was coming to the camp-fire, and if her husband should see him, she knew there would be trouble. What sort of trouble or how far it might extend she did not try to imagine.

"Hector," she said, as soon as she was near enough for him to hear her, "don't go after the pipe; let us take a moonlight walk along the shore. I believe it is full moon to-night, and we have not had a walk of that sort for ever so long."

"Very good," said her husband, turning to her. "I shall be delighted. I don't care for the pipe, and the cigar would have been good enough if it had not been for the sermon. That would spoil any pleasure. I can't stand that young woman, Harriet; I positively cannot."

"Well, then, let us walk away and forget her," said his wife. "I don't wonder she annoys you."

"If it were only the young woman," thought Mrs. Archibald, as the two strolled away beneath the light of the moon, "we might manage it. But her brother!"

At the next indication of a pause in Corona's discourse the bishop suddenly stood on his feet. "I wonder," he said, "if there is anything the matter with Mrs. Archibald? I will step over to her cabin to see."

"Indeed!" said Corona, rising with great promptness, "I hope it is nothing serious. I will go with you."

Margery was not a rude girl, but she could not help a little laugh, which she subdued as much as possible; Mr. Clyde, who was sitting near her, laughed also.

"There is nothing on earth the matter with Aunt Harriet," said Margery. "They didn't go into the cabin; I saw them walking away down the shore."

"How would you like to walk that way?" he asked. "I think their example is a very good one."

"It is capital," said Margery, jumping up, "and let's get away quickly before she comes back."

They hurried away, but they did not extend their walk down the lake shore even as far as Mr. and Mrs. Archibald had already gone. When they came to the bit of beach behind the clump of trees where the bishop had retired that afternoon to read, they stopped and sat down to watch the moonlight on the water.

Matlack and Mrs. Perkenpine were now the only persons at the camp-fire, for Bill Hammond, as was his custom, had promptly gone to bed as soon as his work was done. If Arthur Raybold had intended to come to the camp-fire, he had changed his mind, for he now stood near his sister's tent, apparently awaiting the approach of Corona and the bishop, who had not found the Archibalds, and who were now walking together in what might have been supposed, by people who did not know the lady, to be an earnest dialogue.

Mr. Matlack was seated on his log, and he smoked, while Mrs. Perkenpine sat on the ground, her head thrown back and her arms hugging her knees.

"Phil," said she, "that there moon looks to me like an oyster with a candle behind it, and as smooth and slippery as if I could jest swallow it down. You may think it is queer for me to think such things as that, Phil, but since I've come to know myself jest as I am, me, I've found out feelin's—"

"Mrs. Perkenpine," said Matlack, knocking the

ashes out of his pipe, "there's a good many things besides moons that I can't swallow, and if it's all the same to you, I'll go to bed."

"Well," she exclaimed, looking after him, "his individdlety is the snapshortest I ever did see! I don't believe he wants to know hisself. If he did, I'm dead sure I could help him. He never goes out to run a camp without somebody to help him, and yet he's so everlastin' blind he can't see the very best person there is to help him, and she a-plumpin' herself square in front of him every time she gits a chance." With that reflection she rose and walked away.

"I tell you, Harriet," said Mr. Archibald, when he and his wife had returned from their walk and were about to enter the cabin, "something must be done to enable us to spend the rest of our time here in peace. This is our camp, and we want it for ourselves. If a good companionable fellow like the bishop or that young Clyde happens along, it is all very well, but we do not want all sorts of people forcing themselves upon us, and I will not submit to it."

"Of course we ought not to do that," said she, "but I hope that whatever you do, it will be something as pleasant as possible."

"I will try to avoid any unpleasantness," said he, "and I hope I may do so, but— By-the-way, where is Margery?"

"I think she must be in bed," said Mrs. Archibald; then stepping inside, she called, "Margery, are you there?"

"Yes, Aunt Harriet," replied Margery, "I am here."

" She must have found it dreadfully stupid, poor girl !" said Mr. Archibald.

The lights were all out in the Archibalds' cabin, and still Miss Raybold and the bishop walked up and down the open space at the farther end of the camp.

" Corona !" exclaimed her brother, suddenly appearing before them, " I have told you over and over again that I wish to speak to you. Are you never going to stop that everlasting preaching and give me a chance to talk to you ?"

" Arthur !" she exclaimed, sharply, "I wish you would not interrupt me in this way. I had just begun to say—"

" Oh, my dear Miss Raybold," cried the bishop, "do not let me prevent you from speaking to your brother. Indeed, it is growing late, and I will not trespass longer on your time. Good-night," and with a bow he was gone.

" Now just see what you have done !" said Corona, her eye-glasses brighter than the moon.

" Well, it is time he was going," said her brother. " I have something very important to say to you. I want your good offices in an affair more worthy of your thoughts than anything else at this moment."

" Whatever it is," she said, turning away from him, " I do not want to hear it now—not a word of it. You have displeased me, Arthur, and I am going to my tent."

CHAPTER XXV

A MOONLIGHT INTERVIEW

Mrs. Archibald retired to her cabin, but she did not feel in the least like going to bed. Her husband had long been asleep in his cot, and she still sat by the side of the little window looking out upon the moon-lighted scene ; but the beauty of the night, if she noticed it at all, gave her no pleasure. Her mind was harassed and troubled by many things, chief among which was her husband's unfinished sentence in which he had said that he would try to avoid any unpleasantness, but at the same time had intimated that if the unpleasant thing were forced upon him he was ready to meet it.

Now, reason as she would, Mrs. Archibald could not banish from her mind the belief that Arthur Raybold would come to their camp some time during the next day. In fact, not having heard otherwise, she supposed he had come to the camp-fire that night. She was filled with anger and contempt for the young man who was determined to force himself on their party in this outrageous manner, and considered it shameful that their peaceful life in these woods had been so wickedly disturbed. No wonder she did not want to sleep ; no wonder she sat at the window thinking and thinking.

Presently she saw some one walking over the open space towards the cabin, and she could not fail to recognize the figure with the long stride, the folded arms, and the bowed head. He passed the window and then he turned and repassed it, then he turned and walked by again, this time a little nearer than before.

" This is too much !" said Mrs. Archibald. " The next thing he will be tapping at her window. I will go out and speak my mind to him."

Opening the door very softly, and without even stopping to throw a shawl over her head and shoulders, Mrs. Archibald stepped outside into the night. Raybold was now at a little distance from the cabin, in the direction of Camp Roy, and was just about to turn when she hurried up to him.

" Mr. Raybold," she said, speaking low and rapidly, " if you possessed a spark of gentlemanly feeling you would be ashamed to come into this camp when you have been ordered out of it. My husband has told you he does not want you here, and now I tell you that I do not want you here. It pains me to be obliged to speak to any one in this manner, but it is plain that no other sort of speech will affect you. Now, sir, I know your object, and I will not have you wandering up and down here in front of our cabin. I wish you to go to your own camp, and that immediately."

Raybold stood and listened to her without a word until she had finished, and then he said :

" Madam, there has been a good deal of talk about knowing ourselves and showing ourselves to others. Now I know myself very well indeed, and I will show myself to you by saying that when my heart is interested I obey no orders, I pay no attention to mandates of any sort. Until I can say what I have to say I will watch and I will wait, but I shall not draw back."

For the first time in fifteen years Mrs. Archibald lost her temper. She turned pale with anger. "You contemptible scoundrel! Go! Leave this camp instantly!"

He stood with arms folded and smiled at her, saying nothing. She trembled, she was so angry. But what could she do? If she called Mr. Archibald, or if he should be awakened by any outcry, she feared there would be bloodshed, and if she went to call Matlack, Mr. Archibald would be sure to be awakened. But at this moment some one stepped up quickly behind Raybold, and with a hand upon his shoulder, partly turned him around.

"I think," said the bishop, "that I heard this lady tell you to go. If so, go."

"I did say it," said Mrs. Archibald, hurriedly. "Please be as quiet as you can, but make him go."

"Do you hear what Mrs. Archibald says?" asked the bishop, sternly. "Depart, or—"

"Do you mean to threaten me?" asked Raybold.

The bishop stepped close to him. "Will you go of your own accord," he asked, "or do you wish me to take you away?"

He spoke quietly, but with an earnestness that impressed itself upon Raybold, who made a quick step backward. He felt a natural repugnance, especially in the presence of a lady, to be taken away by this big man, who, in the moonlight, seemed to be bigger than ever.

" I will speak to you," said he, "when there are no ladies present." And with this he retired.

" I am so much obliged to you," said Mrs. Archibald. " It was a wonderful piece of good fortune that you should have come at this minute."

The bishop smiled. "I am delighted that I happened here," he said. "I heard so much talking this evening that I thought I would tranquillize my mind by a quiet walk by myself before I went to bed, and so I happened to see you and Raybold. Of course I had no idea of intruding upon you, but when I saw you stretch out your arm and say 'Go !' I thought it was time for me to come."

"I feel bound to say to you," said Mrs. Archibald, "that that impertinent fellow is persisting in his attentions to Miss Dearborn, and that Mr. Archibald and I will not have it."

"I imagined that the discussion was on that subject," said the bishop, "for Mr. Clyde has intimated to me that Raybold has been making himself disagreeable to the young lady."

" I do not know what we are going to do," said Mrs. Archibald, reflectively ; "there seems to be no way of making an impression upon him. He is like his sister—he will have his own way."

" Yes," said the bishop, with a sigh, "he is like his sister. But then, one might thrash him, but what can be done with her ? I tell you, Mrs. Archibald," he said, turning to her, earnestly, "it is getting to be unbearable. The whole evening, ever since you left the camp-fire, she has been talking to me on the subject of mental assimilation — that is, the treatment of our ideas and thoughts as if they were articles of food—intellectual soda biscuit, or plum pudding, for instance—in order to find out whether our minds can digest these things and produce from them the mental chyme and chyle necessary to our intellectual development. The discourse was fortunately broken off for to-night, but there is more of it for to-morrow. I really cannot stand it."

"I wouldn't stand it," said Mrs. Archibald. "Can't you simply go away and leave her when she begins in that way?"

The bishop shook his head. "No," he said, "that is impossible. When those beautiful eyes are fixed upon me I cannot go away. They charm me and they hold me. Unless there is an interruption, I must stay and listen. The only safety for me is to fly from this camp. At last," he said, smiling a little sadly, "I am going to go. I did not want to do this until your camp broke up, but I must."

"And you are really going to - morrow?" she asked.

"Yes," he said. "I have positively decided upon that."

"I am sorry to hear it," she said. "Good-night."

When Mrs. Archibald entered her cabin she found her husband sleeping soundly, and she again sat down by the window. There was no such thing as sleep for her; her mind was more tossed and troubled than it had been before she went out. The fact that the bishop was going away made the matter worse, for just as she had found out that he was willing to help her, and that he might be able to keep Raybold away from them without actual violence—for she saw that the young boaster was afraid of him—he had told her he must leave, and in her heart she did not blame him. With great fear and anxiety she looked forward to the morrow.

It was about two o'clock when Mrs. Archibald suddenly arose from her seat by the window and lighted a candle. Then she pulled down the shades of the windows, front and back, after which she went to her husband's cot and put her hand upon his shoulder.

" Hector," said she, " wake up."

In a moment Mr. Archibald was staring at her. " What is the matter ?" he exclaimed. " Are you sick ?"

" No," said she, " but I have something very important to say to you. I want you to get up and go away with me, and take Margery."

Mr. Archibald sat up in bed. He was now in full possession of his senses. " What !" said he, " elope ? And where to ?"

" Yes," said she, " that is exactly what I mean, and we will go to Sadler's first, and then home."

" Do you mean now ?" said he.

" Yes—that is, as soon as it is light," she replied.

" Are you positively sure you are awake, Harriet ?" asked Mr. Archibald.

" Awake !" she said. " I have not been asleep to-night. Don't you see I am dressed ?" And

P   225

she drew a chair to the bedside and sat down. "I know more about what is going on than you do, Hector," she said, "and I tell you if we stay any longer in this camp, there is going to be great trouble. That young Raybold pays no attention to what you said about keeping away from us. He comes here when he pleases, and he says he intends to come. I asked you to take a walk with me this evening because I saw him coming to the camp-fire and I knew that you would resent it. To-night I saw him walking up and down in front of our cabin, and I believe he intended to try to speak to Margery. I went out to him myself, and he was positively insulting. If the bishop had not happened to come up, I believe he would have stayed here and defied me. But he made him go.

"Now that you know this, Hector, it is very certain that there will be trouble between you and that young man, and I do not want that. And, besides that, there is his sister; she is as determined to preach as he is to speak to Margery. The bishop says he can't stand her any longer, and he is going away to-morrow, and that will make it all the worse for us—especially for you, Hector. I cannot endure this state of things; it has made me so nervous I cannot get to sleep, and, besides, it is not right for us to keep Margery where she must be continually guarded from such a man. Now it may seem foolish to run away, but I have thought over the matter for hours and hours, and it is the only thing to do; and what is more, it is very easy to do. If we announce that we are going, we will all go, and the chief cause of quarrels and danger will go with us. I know you, Hector ; you will not stand his impertinence.

" It will be daylight between three and four o'clock, and we three can start out quietly and have a pleasant walk to Sadler's. It is only four miles, and we can take our time. We need not carry anything with us but what we choose to put in our pockets. We can pack our bags and leave them here, and Mr. Sadler will send for them. When we get there we can go to bed if we like, and have time enough for a good sleep before breakfast, and then we can take the morning stage and leave this place and everybody in it. Now please don't be hasty and tell me all this is foolish. Remember, if you stay here you have a quarrel on your hands, and I shall have hours of misery until that quarrel is settled ; and no matter how it is settled, things will be disagreeable afterwards."

" Harriet," said Mr. Archibald, suddenly twisting himself so that he sat on the side of the bed, " your idea is a most admirable one. It suits me exactly. Let us run away. It is impossible for us to do anything better than that. Have you told Margery ?"

" No," she answered, " but I will go to her at once."

" Be quick and quiet, then," said her husband, who had now entered fully into the spirit of the adventure ; " nobody must hear us. I will dress, and then we will pack."

" Margery," said Mrs. Archibald, after three times shaking the sleeping girl, " you must get up.

Your uncle and I are going away, and you must go with us."

Margery turned her great eyes on Mrs. Archibald, but asked no questions.

"Yes," said Mrs. Archibald, "we cannot stay in this camp any longer, on account of Mr. Raybold and various other things. Matters have come to a crisis, and we must go, and more than that, we must slip away so that the others may not go with us."

"When?" asked Margery, now speaking for the first time.

"As soon as it is daylight."

"So soon as that?" said the girl, a shadow on her brow which was very plain in the light of the candle which Mrs. Archibald had brought with her. "Surely not before breakfast?"

"Margery," said Mrs. Archibald, a little sharply, "you do not seem to understand—you are not awake; we must start as soon as it is light. But we cannot discuss it now. We are going, and you must go with us. You must get up and pack your things in your bag, which we shall send for."

Suddenly a light came into Margery's eyes and she sat up. "All right," said she, "I will be ready as soon as you are. It will be jolly to run away, especially so early in the morning," and with that she jumped out of bed.

CHAPTER XXVI

A LITTLE more than an hour after Mrs. Archibald had made known her project to her husband the three inhabitants of the cabin stole softly out into the delicate light of the early dawn.

Mr. Archibald had thought of leaving a note for Matlack, but his wife had dissuaded him. She was afraid that the wrong person might get hold of it.

"When we are safely at Sadler's," she said, "we can send for our bags, with a note to Matlack. It will not matter then who knows." She had a firm belief in the power of the burly keeper of the inn to prevent trouble on his premises.

With careful but rapid steps the little party passed along the open portion of the camp, keeping as far as possible from the tent wherein reposed Corona and Mrs. Perkenpine, and soon reached the entrance of the wood road. Here it was not quite so light as in the open, but still they could make their way without much trouble, and after a few minutes' walking they felt perfectly safe from observation, and slackening their pace, they sauntered along at their ease.

The experience was a novel one to all of them ; even Mr. Archibald had never been in the woods so early in the morning. In fact, under these great trees it could scarcely be said to be morning. The young light which made its uncertain way through the foliage was barely strong enough to cast a shadow, and although these woodland wanderers knew that it was a roadway in which they were walking, that great trees stood on each side of them, with branches reaching out over their heads, and that there were bushes and vines and here and there a moss-covered rock or a fallen tree, they saw these things not clearly and distinctly, but as through a veil. But there was nothing uncertain about the air they breathed ; full of the moist aroma of the woods, it was altogether different from the noonday odors of the forest.

Stronger and stronger grew the morning light, and more and more clearly perceptible became the greens, the browns, and the grays about them. Now the birds began to chatter and chirp, and squirrels ran along the branches of the trees, while a young rabbit bounced out from some bushes and went bounding along the road. This early morning life was something they had not seen in their camp, for it was all over before they began their day. There was a spring by the roadside, which they had noticed when they had come that way before, and when they reached it they sat down and ate some biscuit which Mrs. Archibald had brought with her, and drank cool water from Mr. Archibald's folding pocket-cup.

The loveliness of the scene, the novelty of the experience, the feeling that they were getting away from unpleasant circumstances, and in a

perfectly original and independent fashion, gave
them all high spirits. Even Mrs. Archibald, whose
sleepless night might have been supposed to interfere with this morning walk, declared herself
as fresh as a lark, and stated that she knew now
why a lark or any other thing that got up early
in the morning should be fresh.

They had not left the spring far behind them
when they heard a rustling in the woods to the
right of the road, and the next moment there
sprang out into the open, not fifty feet in front of
them, a full-grown red deer. They were so startled by this apparition that they all stopped as if
the beautiful creature had been a lion in their
path. For an instant it turned its great brown
eyes upon them, and then with two bounds it
plunged into the underbrush on the other side of
the road. Mrs. Archibald and Margery had never
before seen a deer in the woods.

The young girl clapped her hands. "It all reminds me of my first night at the opera!" she
cried.

Two or three times they rested, and they never
walked rapidly, so it was after five o'clock when
the little party emerged into the open country
and approached the inn. Not a soul was visible
about the premises, but as they knew that some
one soon would be stirring, they seated themselves in three arm-chairs on the wide piazza to
rest and wait.

Peter Sadler was an early riser, and when the
front hall door was open he appeared thereat, rolling his wheeled chair out upon the piazza with a
bump—though not with very much of a bump,

for the house was built to suit him and his chair. But he did not take his usual morning roll upon the piazza, for, turning his head, he beheld a gentleman and two ladies fast asleep in three great wicker chairs.

"Upon my soul !" he exclaimed. "If they ain't the Camp Robbers !" At this exclamation they all awoke.

Ten minutes after that the tale had been told, and if the right arm of Mr. Sadler's chair had not been strong and heavy it would have been shivered into splinters.

"As usual," cried the stalwart Peter, "the wrong people ran away. If I had seen that bicycle man and his party come running out of the woods, I should have been much better satisfied, and I should have thought you had more spirit in you, sir, than I gave you credit for."

"Oh, you mistake my husband altogether !" cried Mrs. Archibald. "The trouble with him is that he has too much spirit, and that is the reason I brought him away."

"And there is another thing," exclaimed Margery. "You should not say Mr. Raybold and his party. He was the only one of them who behaved badly."

"That is true," said Mrs. Archibald. "His sister is somewhat obtrusive, but she is a lady, gentle and polite, and it would have been very painful to her and as painful to us had it been necessary forcibly to eject her brother from our camp. It was to avoid all this that we—"

"Eloped," interjected Mr. Archibald.

The good Peter laughed. "Perhaps you are

right," said he. "But I shall have a word with that bicycle fellow when he comes this way. You are an original party, if there ever was one. First you go on somebody else's wedding-journey, and then you elope in the middle of the night, and now the best thing you can do is to go to bed. You can have a good sleep and a nine-o'clock breakfast, and I do not see why you should leave here for two or three days."

"Oh, we must go this morning," said Mrs. Archibald, quickly. "We must go. We really cannot wait until any of those people come here. It makes me nervous to think about it."

"Very good, then," said Peter. "The coach starts for the train at eleven."

Mrs. Archibald was a systematic woman, and was in the habit of rising at half-past seven, and when that hour arrived she awoke as if she had been asleep all night. Going to the window to see what sort of a day it was, which was also her custom, she looked out upon the lawn in front of the house, and her jaw dropped and her eyes opened. There she beheld Margery and Mr. Clyde strolling along in close converse. For a moment she was utterly stupefied.

"What can this mean?" she thought. "How could they have missed us so soon? We are seldom out of our cabin before eight o'clock. I cannot comprehend it!" And then a thought came to her which made her face grow pale. "Is it possible," she said to herself, "that any of the others have come? I must go immediately and find out."

In ten minutes she had dressed and quietly left the room.

When Margery saw Mrs. Archibald descending the piazza steps, she left Mr. Clyde and came running to meet her.

"I expect you are surprised to see me here," she said, "but I intended to tell you and Uncle Archibald as soon as you came down. You see, I did not at all want to go away and not let Mr. Clyde know what had become of me, and so, after I had packed my bag, I wrote a little note to him and put it in a biscuit-box under a stone not far from my window, which we had arranged for a post-office, just the day before."

"A post-office!" cried Mrs. Archibald.

"Yes," said Margery. "Of course there wasn't any need for one—at least we did not suppose there would be—but we thought it would be nice; for, you must know, we are engaged."

"What!" cried Mrs. Archibald. "Engaged? Impossible! What are you talking about?"

"Yes," said Margery, "we are really engaged, and it was absolutely necessary. Under ordinary circumstances this would not have happened so soon, but as things were it could not be delayed. Mr. Clyde thought the matter over very carefully, and he decided that the only way to keep me from being annoyed and frightened by Mr. Ray-bold was for him to have the right to defend me. If he told Mr. Raybold I was engaged to him, that of course would put an end to the young man's attentions. We were engaged only yesterday, so we haven't had any time to tell anybody, but we intended to do it to-day, beginning with you and Uncle Archibald. Harrison came over early to the post-office, hoping to find some sort of a note,

234

and he was wonderfully astonished when he read what was in the one I put there. I told him not to say anything to anybody, and he didn't, but he started off for Sadler's immediately, and came almost on a run, he says, he was so afraid I might go away before he saw me."

"Margery," exclaimed the elder lady, tears coming into her eyes as she spoke, " I am grieved and shocked beyond expression. What can I say to my husband? What can I say to your mother? From the bottom of my heart I wish we had not brought you with us; but how could I dream that all this trouble would come of it?"

"It is indeed a very great pity," said Margery, "that Mr. Clyde and I could not have been engaged before we went into camp; then Mr. Raybold would have had no reason to bother me, and I should have had no trouble with Martin."

."Martin!" cried Mrs. Archibald. "What of him?"

"Oh, he was in love with me too," replied the young girl, "and we had talks about it, and I sent him away. He was really a young man far above his station, and was doing the things he did simply because he wanted to study nature; but of course I could not consider him at all."

"And that was the reason he left us!" exclaimed Mrs. Archibald. "Upon my word, it is amazing!"

"Yes," said Margery; "and don't you see, Aunt Harriet, how many reasons there were why Mr. Clyde and I should settle things definitely and become engaged? Now there need be no further trouble with anybody."

Distressed as she was, Mrs. Archibald could not refrain from smiling. "No further trouble!" she said. "I think you would better wait until Mr. Archibald and your mother have heard this story before you say that."

Mr. Archibald was dressing for breakfast when his wife told him of Margery's engagement, and the announcement caused him to twirl around so suddenly that he came very near breaking a looking-glass with his hair-brush. He made a dash for his coat. "I will see him," he said, and his eyes sparkled in a way which indicated that they could discover a malefactor without the aid of spectacles.

"Stop!" said his wife, standing in his way. "Don't go to them when you are angry. We have just got out of trouble, and don't let us jump into it again. If they are really and truly engaged—and I am sure they are—we have no authority to break it off, and the less you say the better. What we must do is to take her immediately to her mother, and let her settle the matter as best she can. If she knows her daughter as well as I do, I am sure she will acquit us of all blame."

Mr. Archibald was very indignant and said a great deal, but his wife was firm in her counsel to avoid any hard words or bad feeling in a matter over which they had now no control.

"Well," said he, at last, "I will pass over the whole affair to Mrs. Dearborn, but I hope I may eat my breakfast without seeing them. Whatever happens, I need a good meal."

When Mr. Archibald came out of the breakfast-room, his mind considerably composed by hot rolls and coffee, he met Margery in the hall.

"Dear Uncle Archibald," she exclaimed, "I have been waiting and waiting for you. I hope you are not angry. Please be as kind to us as you can, and remember, it was just the same with us as it was with you and Aunt Harriet. You would not have run away from the camp in the middle of the night if you could have helped it, and we should not have been engaged so suddenly if we could have helped it. But we all had to do what we did on account of the conduct of others, and as it is settled now, I think we ought all to try to be as happy as we can, and forget our troubles. Here is Harrison, and he and I both pray from the bottom of our hearts that you will shake hands with him. I know you always liked him, for you have said so. And now we are both going to mother to tell her all about it."

"Both?" said Mr. Archibald.

"Yes," said Margery; "we must go together, otherwise mother would know nothing about him, and I should be talking to no purpose. But we are going to do everything frankly and openly and go straight to her, and put our happiness in her hands."

Mr. Archibald looked at her steadfastly. "Such ingenuousness," he said, presently, "is overpowering. Mr. Clyde, how do you do? Do you think it is going to be a fine day?"

The young man smiled. "I think it is going to be a fine lifetime," said he.

The party was gathered together on the piazza, ready to take the coach. The baggage had arrived from the camp in a cart; but Phil Matlack had not come with it, as he remained to take down his tent and settle affairs generally. They were all sorry not to see him again, for he had proved himself a good man and a good guide; but when grown-up married people elope before day-break something must be expected to go wrong. Hearty and substantial remembrances were left for him, and kind words of farewell for the bishop, and even for Miss Corona when she should appear.

Peter Sadler was loath to part with his guests. "You are more interesting now than ever you were," he said, "and I want to hear all about that hermit business; you've just barely mentioned it."

"My dear sir," said Mr. Archibald, with a solemn visage, "sooner or later Miss Corona Raybold will present herself at this inn on her way home. If you want to know anything about her plan to assist human beings to assert their individualities, it will only be necessary to mention the fact to her."

"Good-bye, then," said Peter, shaking hands with Mr. and Mrs. Archibald. "I don't know what out-of-the-way thing you two will do next, but, whatever it is, I hope it will bring you here."

CHAPTER XXVII

MRS. PERKENPINE DELIGHTS THE BISHOP

IT was the bishop who first appreciated the fact
that a certain air of loneliness had descended
upon the shore of the lake. He had prepared
breakfast at his camp, but as Mr. Clyde did not
make his appearance he went to Camp Rob to
look for him. There he saw Matlack and his assistant busy in their kitchen tent, and Mrs. Perkenpine was also engaged in culinary matters.
He had left Arthur Raybold asleep at Camp Roy,
but of the ladies and gentleman who were usual-
ly visible at the breakfast-hour at Camp Rob he
saw no signs, and he approached Mrs. Perkenpine
to inquire for Clyde. At his question the sturdy
woman turned and smiled. It was a queer smile,
reminding the bishop of the opening and shutting
of a farm gate.

"He's a one-er," said she. "Do you suppose
he could ketch a rabbit, no matter how fast he
ran?"

"Come, now," said the bishop, "he wasn't trying to do that?"

"He was either doin' that, or else he was runnin' away. I seed him early this mornin'—I
wasn't up, but I was lookin' round—and I thought
from the way he was actin' that he'd set a rabbit-

trap and was goin' to see if he'd caught anything, and pretty soon I seed him runnin' like Sam Hill, as if his rabbit had got away from him. But perhaps it wasn't that, and maybe somebody skeered him. Anyway, he's clean gone."

The bishop stood and reflected ; the affair looked serious. Clyde was a practical, sensible fellow—and he was gone. Why did he go ?

" Have you seen any of the Archibalds yet ?" he asked.

" No," said she ; " I guess they're not up yet, though it's late for them. My young woman ain't up nuther, but it ain't late for her."

The bishop walked slowly towards the cabin and regarded it earnestly. After a few minutes inspection he stepped up to the door and knocked. Then he knocked again and again, and hearing nothing from within he became alarmed, and ran to Matlack.

" Hello !" he cried. " Something has happened to your people, or they have gone away. Come to the cabin, quick !"

In less than a minute Matlack, the bishop, and Bill Hammond were at the cabin, and the unfastened door was opened wide. No one was in the house, that was plain enough, but on the floor were four bags packed for transportation.

Matlack looked about him, and then he laughed. " All right," said he ; " there ain't no need of worryin' ourselves. They haven't left a thing of theirs about, everything 's packed up and ready to be sent for. When people do that, you may be sure nothing 's happened to them. They've gone off, and I bet it's to get rid of that young woman's preachin'. But I don't blame them; I don't wonder they couldn't stand it."

The bishop made no reply Remembering his recent conversation with Mrs. Archibald, he believed that, if they had quietly gone away, there was a better reason for it than Miss Raybold's fluency of expression. It was possible that something might have happened after he had retired from the scene the night before, for when he went to sleep Raybold was still walking up and down in the moonlight.

His mind was greatly disturbed. They were gone, and he was left. "What are you going to do?" he asked Matlack.

"Nothin' just now," said the guide. "If they don't send for their things pretty soon, I'll go over to Sadler's and find out what's the matter. But they're all right. Look how careful them bags is strapped up!"

The bishop left the cabin and walked thoughtfully away in the direction of Camp Roy. In two minutes he had made up his mind: he would eat his breakfast—he could not travel upon an empty stomach—and then he would depart. That was imperative.

When he reached the camp he found that Raybold had risen and was pouring out for himself a bowl of coffee. Seeing the bishop approach, the young man's face grew dark, as might have been expected from the events of the night before, and he hurriedly placed some articles of food upon a plate, and was about leaving the stove when the bishop reached him. Raybold turned with a frown, and what was meant to be a glare.

"I shall bide my time," said he, and with his coffee and his plate he retired to a distance.

The bishop smiled but made no answer, and sat down and ate his meal in peace ; then he prepared to depart. He had nothing but a little bag, and it did not take long to put in order the simple culinary department of the camp. When all was done he stood for some minutes thinking. There was a path through the woods which led to the road, so that he might go on to Sadler's without the knowledge of any one at Camp Rob, but he felt that he ought to see Matlack and tell him that he was going. If anything went wrong at Camp Roy he did not wish to be held responsible for it. Mr. Archibald could afford to go away without saying anything about it, but he could not, and, besides, if he should happen to see Miss Raybold it would be far more gentlemanly to tell her that he was going and to bid her good-bye, than to slip off through the woods like a tramp. He would go, that he was determined upon ; but he would go like a man.

When he reached Camp Rob the first person he saw was Miss Raybold, standing near her tent with a roll of paper in her hand. The moment she perceived him she walked rapidly towards him.

"Good-morning," she said. "Did you know that the Archibalds had gone? I never was so amazed in all my life. I was eating my breakfast when a man and a cart drove up to their cabin, and Mrs. Perkenpine, running to see what this meant, soon came back and told me that the family of three had departed in the night, and had sent this cart

for their baggage. I think this was a very uncivil proceeding, and I do not in the least understand it. Can you imagine any reason for this
extremely uncourteous action?"

The bishop could imagine reasons, but he did
not care to state them.

"It may be," he said, with a smile, "that they
discovered that their natures demanded hotel
beds instead of camp cots, and that they immediately departed in obedience to the mandates of
their individualities."

"But in so doing," said Miss Raybold, "they
violated the principles of association. Our scheme
included mutual confidence as well as self-investi-
gation and assertion. I must admit that Mr.
Archibald disappointed me. I think he misunderstood my project. By holding one's self entirely
aloof from humanity one encourages self-igno-
rance. But perhaps our party was somewhat too
large—the elements too many and inharmoni-
ous—and I see no reason why we who remain
should relinquish our purpose. I believe it will
be easier for us to become truly ourselves than
when our number was greater, and so I propose
that we make no change whatever in our plans;
that we live on, for the time agreed upon, exactly as if the Archibalds were here. And now,
if you have a few minutes to spare, I would like
to read you something I wrote this morning before I left my tent. I was awake during the
night, and thought for a long time upon the subject of mental assimilation, the discussion of
which we did not finish last evening, and this
morning, while my thoughts were fresh, I put

them upon paper, and now I would like to read them to you. Isn't there some shady place where we might sit down? There are two camp-chairs; will you kindly place them under this tree?"

The bishop sighed, but he went for the chairs. It would be too hard for him to tell her he was going to leave the camp, and he would not try to do it. He would slip off as soon as he had a chance, and leave a note for her. She would not perhaps like that, but it was the best he could do.

The reading of the paper occupied at least half an hour, and when it was finished, and Corona had begun to make some remarks on a portion of it which she had not fully elaborated, Mrs. Perkenpine approached, and stood before her.

"Well, miss," said she, "I'm off."

Miss Raybold fixed her eye-glasses upon her. "What do you mean?" she asked.

"I'm goin' back to Sadler's," she replied. "Phil's goin', and I'm goin'. He's jest told me that the cart 's comin' back for the kitchen fixin's and his things, and him and Bill Hammond is goin' to Sadler's with it; and if he goes, I goes."

This speech had a very different effect upon its two hearers. Corona was as nearly angry as her self-contained nature would permit; but, although he did not allow his feelings to betray him, the bishop was delighted. Now they must all go, and that suited him exactly.

"It is a positive and absolute breach of contract!" exclaimed Miss Raybold. "You agreed to remain in my service during my stay in camp, and you have no right to go away now, no matter who else may depart."

Mrs. Perkenpine grinned. "That sort of thing was all very well a week ago," said she, "but it won't work now. I've been goin' to school to myself pretty steady, and I've kept myself in a good deal, too, for not knowin' my lessons, and I've drummed into me a pretty good idea of what I be, and I can tell you I'm not a woman as stays here when Phil Matlack's gone. I'm not a bit scary, but I never stayed in camp yet with all greenhorns but me. When I find myself in that sort of a mess, it's my nater to get out of it. Phil says he's goin' to start the fust thing this afternoon, and that's the time I'm goin', and so, if you would like to go, you can send word by that man in the cart to have you and your things sent for, and we can all clear out together."

"Positively," exclaimed Corona, turning to the bishop, "this is the most high-handed proceeding I ever heard of!"

"That's 'xactly what I think," said Mrs. Perkenpine; "it most takes my breath away to think how high-handed I am. Before I knowed myself I couldn't have been that way to save my skin. There didn't use to be any individdlety about me. You might take a quart of huckleberries and ask yourself what it was particular 'bout any one of them huckleberries—'xceptin' it might be green, and it's a long time since I was that way—and you'd know jest as much about that huckleberry as I knowed about myself. Now it's different. It's just the same as if there was only one huckleberry in a quart box, and it ain't no trouble to see all around that."

"I think, Miss Raybold," said the bishop, "that

this good woman has prosecuted her psychical researches with more effect than any of us."

"Bosh!" exclaimed Miss Raybold. "Do you really think I must leave this camp at the dictation of that person?"

"'Scuse me," said Mrs. Perkenpine, "but I'm goin' to scratch things together for movin'. We'll have dinner here, and then we'll pack up and be off as soon as the carts come. That's what Phil says he's goin' to do."

With a satisfied mind and internal gratitude to Mrs. Perkenpine, who had made everything easy for him, the bishop endeavored to make Corona feel that, as her departure from the camp was inevitable, it would be well not to disturb her mind too much about it. But it was of no use trying to console the lady.

"It is too bad," she said; "it is humiliating. Here I believed that I was truly myself; that I was an independent entity; that I was free to assert my individual nature and to obey its impulses, and now I find that I am nothing but the slave of a female guide. Actually I must obey her, and I must conform to her!"

"It is true," said the bishop, musingly, "that although we may discover ourselves, and be greatly pleased with the prospect of what we see, we may not be permitted to enter into its enjoyment, and must content ourselves with looking over the fence and longing for what we see."

Corona faintly smiled. "When we have climbed high enough to see over that fence," she said, "it becomes our duty to break it down."

"When I was in England," said the bishop, "I

saw a fence—an oak fence—which they told me had stood for four hundred years. It looked awfully tough, and it now reminds me of some of the manners and customs of civilization."

"When you were in England," said Corona, "did you visit Newnham College?"

He never had. But she told him that she had been there for two years. "And now," she continued, "there may be time enough before I must pack up my effects to finish what I was going to say to you about approximate assimilations."

CHAPTER XXVIII

WHEN the Archibald party reached the capital city of their State, the four of them took a carriage and drove immediately to the Dearborn residence. Margery had insisted that Mr. Clyde should go with them, so that he and she should present themselves together before her parents. In no other way did she believe that the subject could be properly presented. The Archibalds did not object to this plan ; in fact, under the circumstances, they were in favor of it. During the journey young Clyde had produced a very favorable impression upon them. They had always liked him well enough, and now that they examined his character more critically, they could not fail to see that he was a kind-hearted, gentlemanly young man, intelligent and well educated, and, according to private information from Margery, his family was of the best.

Arrived at the Dearborn door, they found the house in the possession of one female servant, who informed them that Mr. Dearborn was in Canada, on a fishing expedition ; that Mrs. Dearborn had gone to attend some sort of a congress at Saratoga, and that she did not expect to be at home until the following Friday, three days after, which

was the day on which she had expected her
daughter to be brought back to her. This was
disheartening, and the four stood upon the steps
irresolute. Margery ought to go to her mother,
but neither of the Archibalds wished to go to
Saratoga, nor could they despatch thither the
prematurely betrothed couple.

"I know what we must do," said Mrs. Archibald, "we must go home."

"But, my dear," said her husband, "we agreed
to stay away for a month, and the month is not
yet up."

"It doesn't matter," said she. "Kate and her
husband will take us in for the few days left.
When we explain all that we have gone through,
she will not be hard-hearted enough to make us go
to a hotel until Friday; Margery can come with us."

Margery turned upon Mrs. Archibald a pair of
eyes filled with earnest inquiry.

"I know what you want," said Mrs. Archibald.
"No, he can go to a hotel in the town; and I shall
write to your mother to come to us as soon as she
returns; then you two can present yourselves together according to your plans. There is no use
talking about it, Hector; it is the only thing we
can do."

"We shall break our word to the newly married," said her husband. "Isn't there a State law
against that?"

"When we made that arrangement," said his
wife, going down the steps, "we did not know
our individual selves; now we do, and the case is
different. Kate will understand all that when I
explain it to her."

249

They drove back to the station, and took a train for home.

Mr. and Mrs. Bringhurst were sitting in the cool library about nine o'clock that evening; he was reading while she was listening, and they were greatly astonished when they heard a carriage drive up to the front door. During their domestic honey-moon they had received no visitors, and they looked at each other and wondered.

"It is a mistake," said he ; "but don't trouble yourself. Mary has not gone to bed, and she will hear the bell."

But there was no bell; the door was opened, and in came father and mother, followed by a strange young couple.

"It is wonderful!" exclaimed Kate, when at last everybody had been embraced or introduced. "A dozen times during the last week have we talked about the delight it would give us if our father and mother could be here to be entertained a little while as our guests in our own house—for you gave it to us for a month, you know. But we refrained from sending you an invitation because we did not want to cut off your holiday. And now you are here ! The good fairies could not have arranged the matter better."

When all the tales had been told ; when the assertion of individuality and the plans of hermit association had been described and discussed, and the young Bringhursts had told how they, too, without knowing it, had been associate hermits, devoting their time not to the discovery of their own natures, but of the nature of each other, and how perfectly satisfied they had been with the results, it was very late, and young Clyde was not allowed to go out into the darkness to find a hotel.

It was on Thursday afternoon that Mrs. Dearborn arrived at the Archibalds' house. The letter she had received had made her feel that she could not wait until the end of the congress.

"Now, mother," said Margery, when the two were alone together, "you have seen him and you have talked to him, and Uncle Hector has told you how he went to the office of Glassborough & Clyde and found he was really their nephew, and all about him and his family; and you have been told precisely why it was necessary that we should engage ourselves so abruptly on account of the violent nature of Mr. Raybold and the trouble he might cause, not only to us, but to dear Aunt Harriet and Uncle Archibald. And now we come just like two of your own children and put the whole matter entirely into your hands and leave you to decide, out of your own heart, exactly when and where we shall be married, and all about it. Then, when father comes home, you can tell him just what you have decided to do. You are our parents, and we leave it to you."

"What in the world," said Mrs. Dearborn, an hour later, when she was talking to the two married ladies of the household, "can one do with a girl like that? I do not believe dynamite would blow them apart; and if I thought it would I should not know how to manage it."

"No," said Mrs. Archibald, "I am afraid the explosion would be as bad for you as it would be for them."

"Don't try it," said Mrs. Kate. "I take a great interest in that budding bit of felicity ; I consider it an outgrowth of our own marriage and honeymoon. When we sent out that wild couple, my father and mother, on a wedding-tour, we did not dream that they would bring back to us a pair of lovers, who never would have been lovers if it had not been for us, and who are now ready for a wedding - tour on their own account, as soon as circumstances may permit. And so, feeling a little right and privilege in the matter, I am going to ask you, Mrs. Dearborn, to let them be married here whenever the wedding - day shall come, and let them start out from this house on their marriage career. Now don't you think that would be a fine plan? I am sure your daughter will like it, when she remembers what she owes us ; and if Mr. Clyde objects I will undertake to make him change his mind."

When the plan was proposed in full counsel, it was found that there would be no need for the exercise of Mrs. Kate's powers of persuasion.

About ten days after Mrs. Dearborn and Margery had returned to their home, and Clyde had followed, to move like a satellite in an orbit determined by Mrs. Dearborn, Mr. Archibald was surprised, but also very much pleased, to receive a visit from the bishop.

"I could not refrain," said that expansive individual, "from coming to you as soon as circumstances would allow, and, while expressing to you the great obligations under which you have placed me, to confide to you my plans and my prospects.

You have been so good to me that I believe you will be pleased to know of the life work to which I have determined to devote myself."

"I am glad to hear," said the other, "that you have made plans, but you owe nothing to me."

"Excuse me," said the bishop, "but I do. This suit of clothes, sir, is the foundation of my fortunes."

"And well earned," said Mr. Archibald. "But we will say no more about that. Have you secured a position? Tell me about yourself."

"I have a position," said the bishop. "But would you prefer that I tell you of that first, or begin at the beginning and briefly relate to you what has happened since I saw you last?"

"Oh, begin at the beginning, by all means," said Mr. Archibald. "I was sorry to be obliged to leave you all so unceremoniously, and I greatly desire to know what happened after we left."

"Very good, then," said the bishop, "I will give you our history in as few words as I can. On the afternoon after your departure we all went to Sadler's—that is, Miss Raybold and myself and the three guides; for Raybold, when he heard that Miss Dearborn and Mr. Clyde had gone, immediately left for Sadler's, hoping, I think, to find you all there. From what I heard, I think he and Peter Sadler must have had words. At any rate, he discovered that his case was hopeless, and he had himself driven to the station in a carriage, not choosing to wait until our arrival. I have since heard that he has determined to relinquish the law and devote himself to the dramatic arts.

"For some reason or other, Peter Sadler was very glad to see me, and congratulated me heartily on the favorable change in my appearance. He called me his favorite tramp, and invited me to stop at his hotel for a time, but I consented to stay a few days only, for I felt I must go to see the gentleman to whom I wished to engage myself as librarian before my new clothes had lost their freshness. Miss Raybold arranged to stay at Sadler's for a week. She liked the place, and as she had planned to remain away from home for a fortnight, she did not wish to return before the time fixed upon. There were a good many people at Sadler's, but none of them seemed to interest her. She decidedly preferred to talk to Sadler or to me; but although Peter is a jolly fellow, and had some lively conversations with her, he does not seem to care for protracted mental intercourse, and it became so plain to me that she depended upon me, in so large a degree, for companionship and intellectual stimulus, that I did not leave as soon as I intended. It was on Wednesday, in fact, that I steeled my heart and told her that I must positively depart early the following morning, or I could not expect to reach my destination before the end of the week. It was that evening, however, that we became engaged to be married."

"What?" cried Mr. Archibald. "Did you dare to propose yourself to that classic being?"

"No," replied the other, "I cannot, with exactness, say that I did. It would be difficult, indeed, for me to describe the manner in which we arrived at this most satisfactory conclusion. Miss

Raybold is a mistress of expression, and, without moving a hair's-breadth beyond the lines of maidenly reserve which always environ her, she made me aware, not only that I desired to propose marriage to her, but that it would be well for me to do so. There were objections to this course, which, as an honest man, I could not refrain from laying before her, and with my proposition I stated these objections, but they were overruled to my entire satisfaction, and she consented to become Mrs. Bishop."

"Mrs. Bishop?" said the other, inquiringly.

"Oh yes ; Bishop is my name—Henry C. Bishop. It was this name which suggested the title which was playfully given to me. Before our compact was made I had told Miss Raybold all about my family. She did not ask me to do so, but I knew she desired the information, for I had learned to read those beautiful eyes."

"But," said Mr. Archibald, "how about your position ? Did you get the place as librarian ?"

"No," said the other, "I did not ask for it. The question of my vocation has been settled most admirably. There never was a human being more frank, more straightforward and pertinent than Miss Raybold. She knows what she wants, and she makes her plans to get it. With regard to means she is sufficiently endowed, but the life work to which she has devoted herself is far more than she can ever accomplish alone. She needs the constant assistance of a sympathetic and appreciative nature, and that, I am happy to say, I am able to give to her ; and were I to devote myself to any other calling which would interfere with that assistance, I should be doing her a positive wrong. Therefore, should I state it in definite words, I should say that I am to become my wife's private secretary. That is my position, and it suits me admirably; and I may add that Corona assures me that she is thoroughly well pleased. We are to be married in the fall, and I hope it will not be long before we shall have the pleasure of meeting again our former companions of the hermit camp."

"By-the-way," said Mr. Archibald, as his visitor was about to leave, "tell me something of Matlack. I had a great liking for our guide."

"All that I can tell you is this," said Mr. Bishop, smiling: "Not long after we arrived at Sadler's, he went to Peter and asked him if he intended to send out a camping party to any considerable distance. It so happened that a couple of gentlemen were going to a point on the very limits of Sadler's jurisdiction, and with them Matlack petitioned to go, although another guide had been appointed. I made inquiries, and found that, for some reason, probably connected with the persistencies of the female sex, Matlack had become a sort of Daniel Boone and wanted to go away as far as possible from his kind."

"I hope," said Mr. Archibald, "that our example has not made a real hermit of him. Good-bye. I am very sorry that Mrs. Archibald is not at home; but in both our names I wish you and your future wife the best of good fortunes."

"Father," exclaimed Mrs. Kate, when she heard of this interview, "now you must grant me one more favor! Here is another pair of lovers who owe everything to our honey-moon and your wedding-tour. We ought to know them, for we made them what they are. So let us invite them here, and let them be married from this house. I do not believe Miss Raybold has a proper home of her own ; and, in any case, the only way they can pay us what they owe us is to give us the pleasure of seeing them wedded here."

Mr. Archibald rose to his feet. " No, madam !" said he. " I am willing, to a certain extent, to make this house a source of hymeneal felicity, but I draw the line at the bishop. I do not intend that my home shall become a matrimonial factory !"

THE END

By MARIA LOUISE POOL

THE RED-BRIDGE NEIGHBORHOOD. Illustrated
by CLIFFORD CARLETON. $1 50.
IN THE FIRST PERSON. $1 25.
MRS. GERALD. Illustrated. $1 50.
AGAINST HUMAN NATURE. $1 25.
OUT OF STEP. $1 25.
THE TWO SALOMES. $1 25.
KATHARINE NORTH. $1 25.
MRS. KEATS BRADFORD. $1 25.
ROWENY IN BOSTON. $1 25.
DALLY. $1 25.

Novels. Post 8vo, Cloth, Ornamental.

The author's narrative gift is as nearly perfect as one could
wish.—*Chicago Interior.*

Miss Pool's novels have the characteristic qualities of American life. They have an indigenous flavor. The author is on her
own ground, instinct with American feeling and purpose.—*New
York Tribune.*

Miss Pool is one of the most distinctive and powerful of nov-
elists of the period, and she well maintains her reputation in this
instance.—*Philadelphia Telegraph.*

HARPER & BROTHERS, PUBLISHERS
NEW YORK AND LONDON

☞ *Any of the above works will be sent by mail, postage prepaid,
to any part of the United States, Canada, or Mexico, on receipt of
the price.*

By MARY E. WILKINS

SILENCE, and Other Stories. Illustrated. 16mo, Cloth, Ornamental, $1 25.

JEROME, A POOR MAN. A Novel. Illustrated. 16mo, Cloth, Ornamental, $1 50.

MADELON. A Novel. 16mo, Cloth, Ornamental, $1 25.

PEMBROKE. A Novel. Illustrated. 16mo, Cloth, Ornamental, $1 50.

JANE FIELD. A Novel. Illustrated. 16mo, Cloth, Ornamental, $1 25.

A NEW ENGLAND NUN, and Other Stories. 16mo, Cloth, Ornamental, $1 25.

A HUMBLE ROMANCE, and Other Stories. 16mo, Cloth, Ornamental, $1 25.

YOUNG LUCRETIA, and Other Stories. Illustrated. Post 8vo, Cloth, Ornamental, $1 25.

GILES COREY, YEOMAN. A Play. Illustrated. 32mo, Cloth, Ornamental, 50 cents.

Mary E. Wilkins writes of New England country life, analyzes New England country character, with the skill and deftness of one who knows it through and through, and yet never forgets that, while realistic, she is first and last an artist.—*Boston Advertiser.*

Miss Wilkins has attained an eminent position among her literary contemporaries as one of the most careful, natural, and effective writers of brief dramatic incident. Few surpass her in expressing the homely pathos of the poor and ignorant, while the humor of her stories is quiet, pervasive, and suggestive.—*Philadelphia Press.*

It takes just such distinguished literary art as Mary E. Wilkins possesses to give an episode of New England its soul, pathos, and poetry.—*N. Y. Times.*

The pathos of New England life, its intensities of repressed feeling, its homely tragedies, and its tender humor, have never been better told than by Mary E. Wilkins.—*Boston Courier.*

The simplicity, purity, and quaintness of these stories set them apart in a niche of distinction where they have no rivals.—*Literary World*, Boston.

The charm of Miss Wilkins's stories is in her intimate acquaintance and comprehension of humble life, and the sweet human interest she feels and makes her readers partake of, in the simple, common, homely people she draws.—*Springfield Republican.*

HARPER & BROTHERS, Publishers

NEW YORK AND LONDON

☞ *Any of the above works will be sent by mail, postage prepaid, to any part of the United States, Canada, or Mexico, on receipt of the price.*

www.ingramcontent.com/pod-product-compliance
Lightning Source LLC
Chambersburg PA
CBHW030624030726
47497CB00006B/1625